CAUSE OF DEATH

Detective Damien Drake

Book 2

Patrick Logan

Books by Patrick Logan

Detective Damien Drake
Book 1: Butterfly Kisses
Book 2: Cause of Death
Book 3: Download Murder

Insatiable Series
Book 1: Skin
Book 2: Crackers
Book 3: Flesh
Book 4: Parasite
Book 4.5: Knuckles
Book 5: Stitches

The Haunted Series
Book 1: Shallow Graves
Book 2: The Seventh Ward
Book 3: Seaforth Prison
Book 4: Scarsdale Crematorium
Book 5: Sacred Heard Orphanage
Book 6: Shores of the Marrow

This book is a work of fiction. Names, characters, places, and incidents in this book are either entirely imaginary or are used fictitiously. Any resemblance to actual people, living or dead, or of places, events, or locales is entirely coincidental.

Copyright © Patrick Logan 2017
Interior design: © Patrick Logan 2017
All rights reserved.

This book, or parts thereof, cannot be reproduced, scanned, or disseminated in any print or electronic form.

Fifth Edition: January 2018

Cause of Death:
>The injury or disease responsible for initiating the morbid chain of events—whether brief or prolonged—that led to death.

Prologue

THE MAN POURED TWO glasses of scotch. He added a splash of pure ethanol to one of them, stirred it with his finger, then made his way back to the table. As he approached his guest from behind, he forced a smile onto his face.

"It's real nice of you to bring me in," the seated man said loudly. "It's—"

The man laid the two glasses on the table.

"Aw, sorry, didn't know you was back. I was sayin' it's real nice to bring me in. It's colder than a witch's tit out der."

The smile remained on the man's face as he took a seat across from his guest in the torn trench coat.

"Well, Trevor, I think that the drink might warm you up some. Don't know about keeping the witches at bay, however."

Trevor was a dark-skinned man with a receding hairline and a patchy beard that was interspersed with blotches of gray. He had wide-set eyes, which had a habit of darting about nervously.

"Thank you, Mister," Trevor said. "Wha—wha'd you say your name was, again?"

The man smiled and took a sip of his own scotch.

"I didn't."

Trevor eyed him suspiciously, but the call of the drink was too great for him to heed any warning signs. He gulped greedily, wincing as he swallowed.

"I ain't the gay type… I—I—I 'preciate the drink and warm house 'n all, but I ain't doin' no gay shit."

The man chuckled.

"Why is it that everyone thinks a kind gesture is expected to be repaid in some way?"

Trevor took another sip, his eyes darting. Instead of answering the question, he cleared his throat, and said, "This be a real nice place you got. What are you? Some sort of doctor? Lawyer? I saw a place like dis once in a book, it was a rich lawyer's house."

"Something like that," the man said with a smile. He observed that Trevor's glass was nearly empty, and even though he had just sat down, offered, "Would you like another?"

Trevor seemed to consider this for a moment. The crystal rock glass was trembling slightly in his fingerless gloves, but it was unclear if this was from fear, hunger, or just the alcohol.

With a slow blink, Trevor brought the drink to his lips and finished the rest of the pale gold liquid.

"Sure," he replied. When he went to put the glass back on the table, it banged loudly, as if he had misjudged the distance. "Is good shit. I'll have another."

Another came out like *anudder*.

"Yes," the man said, taking a sip of his own scotch. "Yes, it is 'good shit'."

Then he stood and started toward the kitchen. As he went, he said, "I see that your gloves have holes in them—the fingers are missing. Interested in a new pair?"

When he made it to the kitchen, he made sure to make his guest's glass with half ethanol and half scotch this time.

"Why you doing this, man? What's in it for you?"

He sighed, and placed his palms on the marble countertop, closing his eyes as he did. His chest rose and fell with several deep breaths, then, after he had collected himself, he picked up the glass and the pair of leather gloves beside them. Tucking a sweater that he had laid on the counter earlier in the day beneath one arm, he made his way back to the kitchen table and placed all three items in front of his guest.

Trevor did the shifty eye thing again, but this time he didn't immediately grab the drink.

Ah, I thought it might come to this, the host thought. *Sooner than I expected, but here it is. The hesitation before the fall—before total and complete acceptance.*

"Look," he began slowly, pausing to have a sip of his own glass scotch. "I know this seems strange, and I bet it's been a long, long time since someone has shown you this level of kindness, of respect. And you have every right to be suspicious—in fact, I doubt you would have survived on the streets for as long as you have without your instincts. But, I assure you, I want nothing in return for my hospitality."

Trevor grunted.

"Then why you doin' this?" he asked, his words slurred.

The man smirked. Trevor was more astute than he had first thought. The others' inquisitions had stopped at sidelong glances, pursed lips.

It would all end the same way, however, but still…

"Because I know what it's like—I know what it's like to be down on your luck. I was in your position once, a long time ago. But I got out. Built all of what you see around you with perseverance and dedication. And now I'm looking to pay it back."

Trevor squinted at him, his thin lids lowering over bulging eyes.

"Go ahead, have a drink, put the sweater and gloves on. Keep warm. There are no strings attached here."

Suspicious or not, old habits die hard.

And a free drink was nearly impossible to resist.

Trevor gulped greedily at his scotch and then tore his worn gloves off. He slid the leather gloves on and then wiggled his fingers almost seductively.

"Comfortable, aren't they?" the host asked.

Two drinks and twenty minutes later, Trevor could barely keep his eyes open, let alone stand. And yet he gave both a valiant effort.

The host quickly made his way over him before the trench coat-clad man toppled onto the table.

"Here, let me help you," he said. "You can stay here for the night. I have a spare bedroom."

Trevor mumbled something incomprehensible, and the man slipped an arm around his waist, taking the brunt of his weight.

Holding Trevor upright, he led them to a bedroom with decor that more reflected a cheap motel than the rest of his house. Inside, there were two single beds, between them there was a peeling, particle board nightstand atop which stood a clock.

The neon green numbers read 3:34 am.

Trevor said something that could have been *thank you*, but could have just as easily been *fuck you*, as the host lowered him onto the bed.

Without bothering to pull the cheap bedspread back, the host retreated to the doorway and observed the scene.

"Sleep well, my friend," he said as Trevor started to snore. His smile broadened. "Don't worry about anything... you'll be safe here. I promise."

And then he started to laugh.

PART I – Natural Causes

Chapter 1

"How can you be so sure, Mrs. Armatridge?" Damien Drake asked with something akin to a sigh.

The woman across from him fiddled with the pearls that hung loosely around her neck like a rosary. Her heavily mascaraed eyes narrowed.

"I know, trust me, I know."

Drake leaned back in his chair, tucking his hands behind his head.

"I need a little more to go on than a woman's intuition, you understand. I get that you're upset, but I have a business to run. I can't go off and pursue every woman who thinks that their maid is stealing silverware. It wouldn't do me any good to harass people for no reason."

The woman scowled, and then started rooting around in her purse. This made Drake uncomfortable, and he unlaced his fingers and leaned forward in his chair. He slid his right hand under his desk and placed his fingers loosely on the butt of the gun that was taped beneath.

"Mrs. Arma—"

"Here," she said, pulling out a checkbook.

Drake relaxed and took his hand off his pistol.

She scrawled a number on the check, signed it, and tore it off. Drake reached out and took it from her, his eyes scanning the figure.

He tried not to gawk.

"Maybe this will make you reconsider *harassment*, Damien. As you can tell, I'm serious about this. *Very* serious. I want proof that she's stealing, and then I want her arrested."

Drake nodded quickly, and then put the check in the top drawer of his desk, sliding it beneath the half-empty bottle of Johnny Red.

"I understand your concerns, Mrs. Armatridge, and I can see that you are a woman of conviction. I have no issue moving forward with our professional relationship. But to do so, I'm going to need more than a check."

A razor-thin eyebrow extended high up her forehead. Drake tried to suppress a smile. Mrs. Armatridge's eyebrow looked like a paperclip trying to find solace in her white perm.

"Such as?"

"I'm going to need a set of keys, and codes to any alarms that you might have. I also need a complete itinerary and schedule—for you, your husband, and the maid. To the minute. I want to know when you guys are home, but more importantly, I need to know when you *aren't* going to be there."

The woman fiddled with her necklace again. Despite her previous gesture, and the check, Drake could see that she had become nervous.

And that had been his intention—to let her know just how serious things were about to get. Spying on people, even those you loved, family, had a tendency to end in strife.

"Why do you need keys?" she asked.

"I need to set up surveillance—cameras and what not."

Drake expected to surprise the woman with this comment, but if anything it seemed that the opposite was true.

It seemed to offer comfort.

"And you'll show me everything you record? *Everything?*"

Drake nodded.

"Of course. I'll show the tapes to you, and only you. And when—*if*—we see anything illegal, we'll inform you immediately. I have to admit, though, that these things don't always work out as planned. If, after two weeks, we don't see anything out of the ordinary, we'll pull the cameras and then sit down and have another chat."

The woman nodded.

"Good."

"But," Drake began hesitantly, "sometimes with these cameras, we pick up things that are... how can I say this delicately... not *just* theft. Things that are outside the realm of what one might consider ordinary. Before we move forward, you need to be aware of this and let me know what you want me to do with such videos, should they be recorded. Of course, at *Triple D Investigations*, you can be assured of our complete discretion."

The woman smiled, and Drake suddenly felt slimy. He had a sneaking suspicion that Mrs. Armatridge wasn't only concerned with missing spoons and forks. There was something else that she wanted to catch on video.

"Show me," she said quietly. "I want to see *everything*."

Be careful what you wish for, Drake thought. With a nod, he stood, offered the woman a tired smile and shook her hand.

"Thank you, Mrs. Armatridge. Please provide Screech with the information and keys I requested before you leave."

The woman thanked him back and then left his office.

"And close the door behind you, please!" he shouted, and the woman obliged.

When she was gone, Drake reached into his desk drawer and pulled out the check. He could barely believe it.

Ten grand for a job like this? It had to be some sort of joke.

Leaving the NYPD and starting the small PI outfit, first on his own and then with Screech whom he had found online, had been meant as a stop-gap measure, a way to earn some petty cash while things cooled off at the precinct.

Before he could apply to be a detective again.

After all, Sergeant Rhodes couldn't be around forever, could he?

He held the check up to the light, confirming its legitimacy.

But with money like this...

Drake chuckled, put the check back, then retrieved the bottle of whiskey and poured himself two fingers.

If anything deserved a celebration, it was this.

While he sipped, his mind wandered back to his bug-eyed ex-boss. Instead of searching for Sergeant Rhodes, however, when he turned on the computer, it was his own name that he Googled.

Two articles came up, both written by the same man: Ivan Meitzer.

The first was the Skeleton King expose that he himself had been the informant for, which despite being more than a year old was still the top hit, and the second was the one that Ivan had published shortly after they had captured the Butterfly Killer.

Drake had promised Chase that he wouldn't do the expose despite the debt he owed to Ivan, but it hadn't mattered; someone had gone ahead and spilled the beans, and it had predictably painted Drake in a less than favorable light. When Screech had first brought the article to his attention, he had gone on a rampage wondering who had been the source— Detective Simmons? Yasiv? The bastard Sergeant Rhodes himself? *Chase?*—but after his rage fizzled, he came to realize that it didn't matter who had broken their silence. It was out, and that's what counted.

Drake read the headline for what felt like the thousandth time.

Veteran NYPD Detective breaks all the rules in pursuit of the Butterfly Killer.

He shook his head.

Drake resisted the temptation to read the article again, and instead found himself searching for "NYPD Detective Chase Adams", as was his habit.

One of the first results was Chase smiling broadly, a plaque held in both hands. Standing behind her was Sergeant Rhodes, his weasely eyes poking out from behind round spectacles.

Detective Chase Adams makes First Grade detective in record time, the heading beneath the photo read.

Drake smiled.

After everything that they had been through together, he was happy for her. And a little proud.

He was staring at her image when the door to his office opened, and Screech burst in. Tall, thin and wiry, Steven Horner aka Screech, was in his mid-twenties, but acted as if he had just entered his teenage years. His hair was shaved on the sides with a swooping pompadour on top, which made his face appear even more narrow. His thin goatee didn't help him look any less like a Planter's peanut, either.

"Well, that shit was interesting," Screech said as he bounded toward him.

Screech also had a problem with walking; he simply hadn't seemed to master the art of it. He either bounded, skipped, sprinted, or sauntered.

He never walked.

Drake raised an eyebrow and deliberately peered around him.

"Don't worry, the GILF is gone," Screech said. "Listen, you really want me to set up cameras in her house?"

Drake didn't answer right away. Instead, he reached into the drawer and grabbed a second glass, filling it with a splash of scotch and motioning for Screech to grab it.

As he did, Drake laid the check on the desk in plain view.

"For ten grand, we're going to videotape her cat taking a dump, if she so desires," Drake said. Screech laughed, a high-pitched, irritating noise from which Drake imagined that his nickname had been borne, and then he took a sip of his scotch.

"*Salud*," Screech said after he was done tittering. They clinked glasses and both of them drank.

***

Screech left shortly after Mrs. Armatridge with instructions to set up the cameras in her home the following morning when the maid was out doing groceries, the Mr. was out getting his car serviced and the woman herself was at church service. Drake, feeling more than a little buzzed, was just locking his office door, when a shadow appeared in the entrance to *Triple D Investigations*.

"You forget your dental dam, Screech? Because—"

But the door was thrown so wide that it bounced off the back wall and startled Drake. He removed the keys from the lock and whipped around and found himself staring at a lean, light-skinned black man who stood in the entrance.

"Detective Drake?" the man gasped.

Drake's eyes narrowed, and he felt his body tense, preparing for action.

"Nobody's called me that for some time," he said quietly, trying to measure up the other man.

He was young, with neatly cropped, curly black hair and dark circles under his eyes. But for all of his bluster, his pose was non-aggressive.

He was scared.

"But that is you?" the man asked, moving forward.

Drake nodded.

"Yeah, that's me—Damien Drake."

The man took a deep, hitching breath. When he reached into his leather messenger bag slung over one shoulder, Drake instinctively took a step toward him. Scared or not, he wasn't about to be taken by surprise.

But when the man pulled out a folder, Drake felt his body relax and he admonished himself.

You've got to stop doing that. You're going to give yourself a heart attack thinking that everyone is going to pull an Uzi from their purse.

"We're closing, so if this is about a job, come back tomorrow," Drake said.

The man shook his head.

"No, I'm pretty sure you're going to want to see this," he said flatly.

Drake eyed him suspiciously, and when the other man didn't falter, he nodded.

"Fine, step into my office, then."

Chapter 2

THE MAN INTRODUCED HIMSELF as Dr. Edison Larringer, Eddie for short, a pathology resident at NYU. He spoke in the rushed, hurried speech of a man that needed to be somewhere, everywhere, *anywhere* but here.

"How can I help you, Eddie?" Drake asked, sweeping the scotch and empty glasses back into the drawer. Business had been tough to come by, and he wasn't about to turn down his second whale of the day.

And that said nothing of the other niggling fact, his gut reaction that this man had something important to show him.

Eddie didn't answer. Instead, he swallowed hard and placed the folder on the table and spun it around. Drake picked it up and opened it. The first thing he saw was an 8 x 10 photograph depicting a man half on and half off a bed, his neck bent awkwardly beneath him, his face masked in shadows. There was a second photograph beneath the first, and without thinking, Drake held them side by side.

They looked to be copies.

Drake took his time looking at them, his eyes moving from one to another, trying to ascertain what was so important that the young doctor felt the need to burst into his office at half-past six on a Friday evening.

When nothing came to him, and he doubted that nothing would no matter how long he stared, Drake looked at the man across from him, an eyebrow raised.

"I'm not sure—" he began, but Eddie cut him off.

"They're both dead," he said quickly.

"Yes, I can see—"

"But they aren't the same; they're actually different. Look at the clock, it's a different time, and the sweater isn't exactly the same, the first has like this cross stitch pattern while the other has—"

Now it was Drake's turn to interrupt.

"Woah, slow down there partner. Take a deep breath. Go slow. It's late and I'm old."

Eddie's eyes bulged and his mouth twisted as if to say, *How dare you tell me to slow down with something as important as this? Don't you get it? Don't you understand?*

But in the end, the young man did as asked.

When Eddie spoke again, his words came out more slowly. Still fast by any measure, but slower on a relative scale.

"On the left is a photograph from the NYU forensic pathology course exam, the one with the clock that reads 3:41. The one on the right is a copy, but it's a *copy*, if you catch my drift. See the clock? It reads 3:42 am."

Drake turned his attention back to the photographs and noted that what Eddie was saying was true. And yet he still didn't see the significance.

"I see that, but what does it mean? The pictures were taken a minute apart. So what?"

The man took another deep breath.

"Okay, so the one on the left is from the test—we are given the photograph and then supposed to determine possible causes of death, differentials, if you will—and it's a real photograph from a crime scene. I don't know from when, but judging by the decor, it's at least a decade old, maybe even more. It's the same image used every year in the course."

Drake nodded.

"Okay..."

"It's supposed to be a trick; see how the bedspread is all messed up? The first inclination is that there is foul play involved, that there was a fight, an altercation of some sort that caused his death. At least that's what the professor expects your final diagnosis to be. But the real cause of death is much more… *ordinary*. This man just got very drunk and fell out of bed. He was so drunk that he never woke up when his windpipe was closed off—positional asphyxia, it's called."

Drake looked at the photograph, tilting his head off to one side as he squinted. He had never heard of positional asphyxia, but it looked like a very unpleasant way to go.

He would much rather go out with his fists raised.

Drake shook his head and held out the second photograph, the one with the clock reading 3:42.

"And this one?"

Eddie blinked.

"This one is different; it's not the same person, not the same crime. It's been staged."

Drake's eyes narrowed.

"How do you know?"

"It's been made to look like the first one, like the photo from the test, but it isn't the exact same."

Drake felt himself nodding.

"And where did you get this one from?" he asked, shaking the photograph in his right hand.

Eddie suddenly leaned back in his chair, and Drake thought he saw sweat begin to bead on his forehead. For the first time since barging into *Triple D*, the man seemed to be at a loss for words.

Drake waited and eventually Eddie lowered his eyes.

"I stole it," he said quietly.

Drake stared.

It wasn't the revelation he had expected, but it was something.

"From where?"

Again, Eddie hesitated. When he finally answered, his voice was barely audible.

"I stole it from the professor of the course—I stole it from Dr. Beckett Campbell. And I know one thing for certain: that man, the one in the photograph with the clock reading 3:42? He didn't die from positional asphyxia. He was murdered."

Chapter 3

"WAIT A SECOND, YOU *stole* this? From Beckett Campbell?" A look of confusion crossed Eddie's face.

"Yeah, I took it. But the important thing is that this man —" he reached across the table and took the photograph from Drake. "—was *murdered*."

Drake stared at Eddie for a long time before saying anything; he was having a hard time reading the man. Eddie was convincing enough, but this whole thing about stolen photographs from Beckett of all people, of forensic pathology exams, *positional asphyxia*, if that really was a thing, all seemed like a cruel joke.

A setup of some sort, the reason for and the point of, Drake couldn't begin to imagine.

He leaned back in his chair and prepared himself to put this young doctor—if he was in fact a doctor—to the test.

"Alright Eddie, I'm not sure what kind of game you're playing, but I'll play along. But here's the thing: if after I've drunk a fifth of scotch I decide that I don't like the rules of this game, then I'm going to make sure that there is only one loser, and it ain't gonna be me. Got it?"

Eddie screwed up his face and recoiled.

"Game? What are you talking about, *game*? Someone's been murdered. Maybe you haven't been—"

"How'd you find me, Eddie? Of all the private investigators in New York City, you came to me—why? If you're so convinced that the person in the photo was murdered, why don't you go to the police?"

Eddie dropped his gaze and said nothing. Drake grimaced and slid the photograph back into the folder.

"Thanks so much for coming in today, Eddie. But I'm afraid you caught me at a bad time. See, I was just about to go get drunk and celebrate signing a new client—a *real* client," Drake said as he pushed the folder across the desk toward Eddie, an unfamiliar smugness forming on his face. "So if you'll excuse me, I—"

Eddie's eyes shot up.

"Suzan told me about you. Suzan Cuthbert."

Drake froze.

"*What?*" He felt anger immediately start to mount inside him, and his body tensed. "You better watch what you say next, Eddie, or—"

"Suzan's at NYU in her first year of medical school, and she started auditing the forensic pathology resident course," Eddie said leaning away from Drake. "It... uh, the death of her father came up."

Drake leaped to his feet so quickly that his chair toppled behind him.

"You little shit," he seethed. "You come in here with some bullshit story about some sort of copycat killer, then you have the gall to bring up Suzan? Was it that bastard Ivan Meitzer that put you up to this? Revenge for not giving him the Butterfly Killer story?"

Drake saw red and before he even realized what he was doing, he reached across the table and grabbed Eddie by the collar of his white polo shirt. He twisted the material in his hand, bringing Eddie's face to within inches of his own.

"You get the fuck out of here—take your goddamn pictures and get the *fuck* out of here."

He stared into the man's wide eyes as he threatened him. When Eddie tried to look away, he tightened his grip on his shirt until his eyes came back to him.

Only then, after staring at the man's watering eyes for the better part of a minute, did he shove the young doctor away.

Eddie fell back into his chair with a grunt, but then quickly stood, grabbed the folder and shoved it into his messenger back. Then, with a final, wistful glance, Dr. Edison Larringer scrambled out of the office, then through the reception area of Triple D Investigations, leaving both doors wide.

Drake fell back into his chair and sat there, breathing heavily as he watched the man go. Then he reached into his desk and pulled out the bottle of whiskey and glass again.

Seriously? Whoever put the kid up to this must have some serious balls to bring up Suzan.

As he poured himself another drink, the image of the psychiatrist whose nose he had broken outside Suzan's school flashed in his mind.

When I find out who's behind this, I'll break more than his fucking beak.

Drake poured himself another drink, and when his blood pressure started to normalize, he found himself back at his computer again without even thinking about what he was doing.

Only this time he didn't search for his own name, or Chase's, and not even Suzan.

Instead, he searched for Beckett, and a photograph of his friend, smiling widely, his bleach blond hair spiked atop his head, was the first result that popped up.

Chapter 4

Dr. Edison 'Eddie' Larringer left Triple D Investigations with a single thought echoing inside his head.

This was a mistake—this was all a mistake.

He was sweating, he was tired, but most of all he was confused. It dawned on him that everything he had told Drake, everything that had been consuming all of his thoughts for the past six days, had been a fabrication.

It wasn't unthinkable; in fact, it was even plausible given how exhausted he was. Beckett's forensic pathology final exam was on Monday, and he was struggling just to stay afloat. If anything, Eddie was a realist; and if he was being honest with himself, he knew that he wasn't going to pass. And one more fail meant that his entire career as a physician was in jeopardy. Which is why he had, after much moral anguish, broken into Dr. Campbell's office.

He didn't have to take the folder with the photographs that lay on Beckett's desk, which at first had looked like hard copies of the final exam. After all, he didn't *need* them—the USB key he had taken had digital versions embedded within the PowerPoint presentation. That was enough, *more* than enough, for Eddie to pass.

He didn't need the folder.

In fact, he wasn't entirely sure why he had taken it. He just had.

And now Eddie was beginning to think that this had been the biggest mistake of his life.

If only I hadn't looked at the photographs. Things would be different if I had just burned the entire folder.

But he hadn't. And once he looked, it was impossible for him to *un*look.

At first blush, the digital and printed images looked nearly identical.

But they weren't; they were just a little off. And when Eddie searched the Internet for accidental deaths over the last six months, he found the description of one that perfectly matched the image in the folder.

Only that image also matched the one from the course, which, considering the grainy texture of the photo in the PowerPoint, must have been taken years ago.

It wasn't exemplary, it was nearly *exactly* the same. Textbook, in a way that defied logic.

Eddie just couldn't believe that it was a coincidence.

Someone had taken a photograph of a recent crime scene staged to look exactly like the one used in the test.

And the only reason that someone would do this, in his opinion, was to cover up a murder.

Eddie quickly made his way across the parking lot to his worn Cavalier and fumbled with his keys to open the door. It was already dark out, a fact that further added to his anxiety.

Once inside, he sat behind the wheel for several moments before starting the car.

Should *I go to the police as Drake suggested?* He wondered.

That, too, would lead to him failing his exam, of that Eddie was certain. After all, stealing a test from his professor's desk would amount to more than just him staying behind to repeat a year of forensic pathology. NYU took plagiarism, theft, and cheating very, very seriously.

And so did the police.

If he went to the cops and admitted what he had done, it would mean that they would take away his medical license.

Eddie had thought about the bind he had gotten himself into for several sleepless nights. But when the young and pretty Suzan Cuthbert started to audit the class, it looked to him like a solution to his problem had fallen into his lap. After all, everyone knew what happened to Suzan's father, and a little research on his part revealed information about his partner, about Damien Drake.

Surely, the man would help him out, would take him seriously, given that he knew Suzan. What he hadn't planned for was the man's temper.

Eddie's eyes lifted to the rear-view, and he was shocked to realize that he barely recognized his own gaunt features.

"A mistake, this was all a big mistake," he said in a dry croak. "A mistake."

But try as he might, there was no way he could put the image of the man in the sweater, his body hunched over his own neck, out of his mind.

He couldn't *un*see.

It's no coincidence. It can't be.

Eddie reached for his keys and was about to put them in the ignition when a flash of movement in the mirror caught his eye.

"What the—"

But Dr. Edison Larringer didn't even get a chance to finish his sentence. A dark figure rose from the back seat, and a thick piece of rope was wrapped around his throat.

He gasped and reached for the ligature, but it was yanked tight, forcing the back of his head against the headrest. Eddie clawed desperately at the rope, trying to force his fingertips between the twine and the soft tissue of his neck, but it was no use.

It was just too tight.

As he gasped and desperately tried to fill his lungs with fresh air, he saw the door to Triple D Investigations swing open and the man himself stepped out into the parking lot.

Help me! Eddie tried to scream. *Help me, Damien! Help me!*

But no words came out.

And yet despite this, Drake seemed to pause for a moment, his face a sickly yellow in the streetlights, his eyes scanning the parking lot and street beyond.

Please, help me!

Eddie's heart sunk when Damien shook his head and made his way to his own car.

Only seconds later, Dr. Edison Larringer's entire world went dark.

Chapter 5

DR. BECKETT CAMPBELL SQUINTED at his students as he spoke, deliberately meeting each and every one of their stares before continuing.

What had started as an innocent suggestion by Diego for him to teach a class at NYU, had soon grown into a challenge for Beckett. And this challenge had quickly transitioned into something that he liked very much.

Very, *very* much.

Who knew torture could be so enjoyable?

"This is it," he said, drawing the words out dramatically, much like a voice-over for a blockbuster movie trailer. "This one test will determine the rest of your adult life. Fail? You die. Barely pass? Gravely wounded. Pass? You get to diddle dead bodies for eternity. The choice is yours, my disciples."

The pale faces of the students before him almost made Beckett break into full-blown laughter. One boy—Reginald? Was it Reginald? He could never remember the damn students' names—visibly gagged and, for one brief, tantalizing moment, Beckett thought that he was going to vomit on his desk.

But, to his dismay, the boy gulped like a fish out of water and managed to keep it together for the time being.

"I'm just messing with you guys," Beckett said with a chuckle. But the accompanying smile faded when his eyes fell on the only empty seat in the classroom. He searched the room again, trying to figure out which of the eleven residents was missing. "But you know the rules. Keep your eyes on your own paper. I'll put up an image on the projector, you guys read the accompanying paragraph on the sheet in front of you, then follow the instructions. Remember, it's not always about getting the correct diagnosis. It's about getting the right *diagnoses* given the information you have at hand."

The light-skinned black guy—Arnold or Eddie or something like that—he's missing.

He shook his head disapprovingly, but when he noticed the woman sitting off to the right, separate from the other students, his mood lightened. Her face was smoother than the others, as of yet unburdened by the plight of age and a deep understanding of death.

Beckett smiled at her, then to the rest of the class, he said, "Alright, your one hour, my pupils, begins now. One hour for eight cases. Which means that the slides will automatically switch every seven and a half minutes, for you doctors who struggle with long division. Once the image changes, there ain't no goin' back."

With that, Beckett pressed the small button in the lower right-hand corner of the computer screen and the projector flicked to life. He waited for a moment as the projector started to focus, and craned his head around to look at the image.

It showed a man wearing a striped sweater lying on the back third of his head, his chin tucked against his chest in an awkward fashion. Satisfied that this was the correct image, Beckett nodded to himself and was about to turn away when he noticed something that he hadn't seen before.

The sweater was off; he remembered the photograph in his desk drawer, and he was certain that in it the geometric pattern went north/south, not east/west as it was in the image onscreen. Beckett squinted at the image for a moment, trying to think back.

While names eluded him, especially those of the snot-nosed residents, something like this did not. Things related to death remained etched in his brain as if chiseled on a stone tablet.

Something's not right here.

Beckett made a mental note to review the images in his desk drawer after the test was over.

"Get *ascribblin'*, people."

Eyes that had been previously locked on him snapped down, tongues pushed into cheeks, and pencils did, as he had suggested, get *ascribblin'*.

Beckett walked over to the young woman off to the right and kneeled down close to her ear.

"Suze, remember that you're just auditing the course. No need to get all stressed out about it."

Suzan Cuthbert raised her head to look at him, pushing her long brown hair behind her ears before answering. She had a spooked expression on her face, and he wondered if perhaps the course content was too advanced for her.

Too *visceral*.

But then she broke into a smile, revealing a set of perfectly straight, white teeth.

"I'm afraid… I'm afraid It's too easy," she said quietly, and Beckett laughed. He patted her on the shoulder and then went back to his desk. He sat, put his feet up, and pulled a book from his bag.

Enough of this so-called 'reality'*, he thought. Time for something more interesting.*

Then he opened the book to the dog-eared page roughly halfway through and continued reading Ambrose Ibsen's *The Asylum*.

***

Someone nudged Beckett's leg and he startled awake.

"Wha—?" he gasped, and almost fell out of his chair. He righted himself, catching the book as it slid from his chest.

He was staring at Suzan Cuthbert's pretty face, who was looking back at him with a smirk.

Beckett wiped the drool from the corner of his mouth and observed her for a moment, still trying to catch his bearings.

"The test?" she said softly, and Beckett nodded, now remembering where he was. And yet, despite this realization, he was unsure of why she was standing before him. He peeked around and saw that the residents were all still scribbling away at their papers. He turned his gaze to the projector next and noted that the final image—which depicted a charred, crispy corpse—was still up.

"Do you…" *need a break?* He meant to ask, but stopped short when she held out several sheets of paper to him. The right side of his upper lip curled. "You're done?"

Suzan beamed and nodded vigorously.

Beckett eyed her suspiciously.

The thing about the forensic pathology final exam—the written portion, anyway—was that no one ever 'finished'. They just kept on writing until Beckett told them to stop. And even then, there was always one person who he had to go and physically remove the pencil from their hand. Beckett's first thought was that Suzan maybe didn't finish all of the slides, or that she had simply missed the point of the exam, but when his eyes fell on the dense block of text on her paper, and then the smirk on her face, he knew that this wasn't the case.

He knew she was bright, but this was… suspicious.

"Thanks," he said, taking the paper from his hand. Her smiled broadened, and when she turned to leave an idea occurred to him.

"Hey Suze, why don't you stop by my office sometime this afternoon? You have class?"

Suzan thought about this for a moment.

"Only until two-thirty, then I'm free."

Beckett nodded.

"Good, I'm there until four. Swing by, I've got a job for you."

She raised an eyebrow.

"A job?"

"Sure, a job. You know, work. Hard labor. Mining. Landscaping. Mike Rowe's *Dirty Jobs*. See you this afternoon," then he stood, and to the rest of the class, he said, "Alright you so-called doctors, time's up. Stop writing, put your lead peckers down, and hand in your papers."

As expected, the room erupted into groans. One student even went as far as to mutter something about the fact that they still had three minutes left, to which Beckett suggested that they report him to the secret police.

By the time all of the students had handed in their papers, the PowerPoint switched again, momentarily dimming the lighting in the room. Beckett turned his head around and realized that the loop of images had started over again.

And onscreen was the same image of the man, the one with the sweater that, for whatever reason, wasn't quite right.

Chapter 6

DRAKE SLEPT SOUNDLY, AS he did on most nights since he had shot Dr. Mark Kruk. His dreams of Clay and the Skeleton King faded into the background, becoming more white noise than coherent images, something that he could ignore without much effort. Every once in a while he would find himself startled from slumber, and his eyes would focus on the finger bone that he laid on the small table beside his bed as a constant reminder.

While sleeping soundly was a relief, Drake never forgot.

Forgetting would mean that Clay had died without reason. And yet Drake was grateful when he discovered that there was such a thing as remembering without being haunted day and night.

When he finally awoke, around eight-thirty according to the cheap analog clock on the nightside table, he opened his eyes, clucked his tongue, and waited for his eyes to focus on the small, dice-sized bone.

More than once he had thought about going to Beckett and asking him to see if he could do a DNA test on the bone itself, to find out where Kenneth Smith had acquired it from—*who* he had acquired it from. Even though Ivan had been the one to unceremoniously throw it on the table at Patty's Diner, Drake had no doubt as to whom had given it to him.

But he had resisted the urge.

Drake wasn't so proud to admit that he couldn't admit that he was scared.

Scared of the nightmares returning.

So instead, every morning, after showering and dressing, he would slip the bone into his pocket and carry it around with him, a morbid reminder of what happened when you stopped paying attention, when you got so stuck in your ways that you can't see anything new.

One day, he told himself, *one day I'll find out where this came from. And when I do, I'll find you, you bastard. I'll find the man who really killed Clay. The real Skeleton King.*

Drake groaned and pulled himself out of bed. He was surprised that his head was no longer fuzzy and congested upon waking, something else, like the lack of nightmares, that he was slowly becoming accustomed to.

While he still very much enjoyed his Johnny Red, and dreamed of the Blue that Ken had offered him that rainy night, he had cut his consumption back to a level that ensured he wouldn't have to wait until noon for the alcoholic fog to finally clear.

Drake went straight to the shower. As water sluiced off of him, he found his thoughts wandering to Chase of all people.

About how he had thrown himself on the grenade that was the Butterfly Killer case, sacrificing himself to make sure that she could live on.

And live on she did.

A smile crossed his face, thinking about the fact that she had already become a first-grade detective.

It's almost time, he thought, *almost time to reach out to her, to speak again.*

The truth was, he liked Chase. He liked her no-nonsense approach to detective work, to her life, to *him* of all people. She was the only one back at 62nd that he missed. Not Simmons, not Yasiv, and definitely not Rhodes.

Just Detective Chase Adams.

Well, Clay, too, but that was a different matter entirely.

Drake also admired the way that Detective Adams was willing to fudge the rules, just a wee smidgen, in order to keep the people of New York City safe.

After toweling off, Drake pulled on a pair of jeans and a t-shirt.

There were aspects of his old life that he missed, but wearing the same damn chinos and sport coat wasn't one of them.

And if checks like the one Mrs. Armatridge had given him kept on coming, well, shit, the things he *did* miss about being a detective might soon be forgotten.

Thoughts of the elderly woman brought an image to mind. He was sitting across from her, her hands nervously fondling comically large pearls that hung around her neck.

"My maid…" she began, her voice acquiring the watery quality consistent with daydreams, "she's been killing people."

Mrs. Armatridge took a folder out of her over-sized purse and handed it over to him. Drake knew before he even opened the folder that it wasn't going to be filled with images of ancient looking silverware.

It was a photograph of a dead man, his neck bent awkwardly beneath him.

"It's the same, but *different*," Mrs. Armatridge said, her voice deepening. "I stole it from Beckett."

With the word Beckett, her voice changed completely; it was the young doctor's voice, now.

Drake shook his head.

Not my problem now, he thought. *It's someone else's problem. Let the boys—and girls—in blue figure it out.*

Drake grabbed his phone from the kitchen and switched it on. He was still learning how to use the damn thing—his fingers seemed too big for the electronic keyboard—but he had to admit that the outfit that Screech had hooked him up with was pretty impressive.

And a dozen times more useful than his last one.

"Speak of the devil," he muttered as a text message from Screech popped on the screen.

Arriving at Mrs. Armatridge's now. Can't expect that this is going to take more than a few hours.

Drake nodded to himself and then started to type his reply.

I've got nuggets to do today. I'll jingle you.

He cursed.

Jingle you? What the hell? Screech wrote back.

Join, Drake corrected. *I'll join you.*

Screech's reply was instantaneous: a laughing emoticon.

Drake frowned.

Useful, and a colossal waste of time.

Chapter 7

TRUE TO HER WORD, SUZAN Cuthbert arrived at Beckett's office just before three-thirty in the afternoon. He had completed marking three of the eleven exams—they all passed, some by the skin of their teeth—and was taking a break to look over Suzan's own when there was a knock at his door.

"Come on in," he said, without looking up.

Suzan had nailed the first case. She had written the differential as "homicide", but the main diagnosis, the *correct* cause of death, was listed as *positional asphyxia*, likely due to alcohol intoxication.

A smile crossed his face.

She was good. *Really* good. Most of his residence had gotten the answer correct—it was, after all, the easiest of the eight cases—but she was the only one of first three he had graded to have noticed the half empty bottle of vodka peeking out from beneath a corner of the messy bedspread.

"Dr. Campbell? You wanted to see me?" a small voice asked.

Beckett folded the test paper on top of the stack of others and smiled warmly.

"Just Beckett, Suze," he said. "And come in, take a seat."

Suzan did as was bid and looked up at him in anticipation. If it had been anyone else before him, Beckett would have reveled in her minor discomfort, allowed her to sit there while he tidied his desk, picked his nose, scratched his balls—did *whatever* to prolong the sensation.

It wasn't that he was an asshole; rather, it wasn't that he was *just* an asshole—there was a method to his madness. Years of working with the dead had taught him that being uncomfortable made one work more quickly, which can lead to missing potential evidence or cause of death differentials. As did shock. It was his goal to prepare his students for both, which is the reason why he treated them as he did.

And, besides, it was hella fun doing it.

"I want you to be my TA, Suzan," he said quickly.

Suzan's eyes brightened.

"TA? Seriously? I'm not sure—"

Beckett cut her off.

"Do you think I'm a good doctor, Suzan? I don't mean to toot my own horn, but I'm one of three Senior Medical Examiners in NYC—the youngest of the three, I might add—and, as you may or may not be aware, I'm a professor at NYU."

Suzan started to flush and looked about to say something, but Beckett stopped her by leaning forward.

"I knew Clay—he was a great man. So before you say anything, know this: I'm not asking you to be my TA because of him. I'm asking because of *you*. I think you're smart and going to make one hell of a doctor one day. The way I figure it, if I can get you in here now, maybe one day you'll come work for the Medical Examiner's office. So, before you say some '*I need to think about it*' or some such nonsense, I'm just going to go ahead assume the answer is yes."

Beckett stood quickly and reached for his coat on the back of his chair. He put it on, and then pulled a wool cap from the pocket and pulled it over his ears. It was only September, but it seemed that the last vestiges of a warm summer were fleeing them quickly.

The weather prognosticators, as brutal as they were most of the time, were predicting the first snowfall to come in the third week of September.

"And because that answer is yes, your first job is to grade these papers," he said, passing the pile of exam papers to her. Suzan appeared flustered, embarrassed, and a little confused, and several of the tests fell to the floor. "I've done most of them, but finish up the rest, would you?"

Beckett was at the door when Suzan finally managed to speak.

"B—b—but, where's the solution sheet?"

Beckett, his back to her, smiled.

"Look at your test for the solutions," he said, then left Suzan alone in his office.

Chapter 8

MRS. ARMATRIDGE—WHOSE FIRST name Drake learned from the check that he had promptly deposited was Greta—lived in a large, plain looking semi-detached home in upper Manhattan. Drake noticed Screech's car, a brand new Tesla, parked across the street, and he pulled his Crown Vic behind it. Rubbing his hands together to warm them, he walked quickly to the door.

It was unlocked, and he stepped inside without knocking.

Modest from the exterior, the inside of Greta Armatridge's home was a different animal altogether.

It was like stepping into an alternate dimension—a dimension in which everything had been coated in precious metal or rare, tightly woven fabrics.

The first thing he noticed was the crown molding that outlined a twelve-foot high coffered ceiling; the second was the original flooring that was so buffed he could make out his own reflection in them. Spread out across the floor were pieces of hulking furniture adorned with intricate, hand carved arms and legs. The maroon walls were covered in mirrors of various sizes and shapes, and what Drake suspected were original oil paintings wrapped in frames of gilded gold.

After he overcame his shock of the discrepancy of the interior versus exterior of Greta's home, Drake cleared his throat and hollered, "Screech? You here?"

The man's head poked out from behind a staircase, eyes wide.

"Jesus, you scared the shit of me. Ever think of knocking?" Drake's eyes narrowed.

"Never mind. Anyways, wrapping up here. Just setting up the last camera. Wanna give me a hand?"

Drake said sure and made his way toward Screech.

The staircase that his partner had been tucked behind was large and ornate, much like everything in the house, and he was using the underside of the stairs themselves to disguise a camera the size of a silver dollar.

"That's it?" Drake asked, marveling at the tiny recording device.

"Yep, that's it. Already set up three others. One in the kitchen, one in the office, and one in the bedroom, of course."

Drake raised an eyebrow at this, remembering his conversation with Mrs. Armatridge.

Sometimes with these cameras, we pick up things that are... how can I say this delicately... not just theft. Things that are outside the realm of what one might consider ordinary, he had warned her.

And what better place to record such things than in the bedroom?

"Hold the chair, will you?" Screech asked.

Drake frowned at the sight of the man's dusty runners soiling the cushion of what looked like a chair that a museum curator might plant his ass after a long day and everyone had gone home.

Screech leaned forward, pressing the camera into the underside of the dark, wooden staircase.

"Go over there by the couch, let me know if you can see it or not."

Drake backed up several paces, and as he did, he was amazed to see that the camera disappeared, blending into the wood, becoming a knot or other such imperfection in the natural surface.

"Wow," he said. "I wouldn't even know it's there."

"That's kinda the point," Screech said with a smile. He leaned forward and pressed a hidden button on the camera. A small red light came on, but then blinked out a second later.

"There," he said, hopping down from the chair. He proceeded to slap some of the dust off the dark green velvet cushion. "All set."

"That's it?" Drake asked. It all seemed almost too easy.

Too easy for ten grand, anyway.

Screech tilted his head to one side and pushed his lips upward.

"That's it. Pass me your phone, and I'll set it up."

Drake reached into his pocket and pulled out his cell phone. He handed it over, but Screech immediately handed it back.

"The password."

Drake smiled and typed in the four-digit code to unlock it before handing it back.

What had Chase said? Ten thousand possible combinations... Yeah, we should meet up again, Drake thought.

Enough time had passed that being seen with him wouldn't damage her career.

Screech spent several minutes doing something with Drake's phone tilted so that only he could see, before passing it back.

"There you go," he said. Drake looked down at his phone and was surprised to find that his screen had been divided into quadrants. The first three showed scenes from the house—the kitchen, office, and bedroom—while the fourth was showing both Screech and himself. Out of habit, Drake waved a hand in the air and watched as his digital representation mirrored his movements. The picture was crystal, pristine, and the delay was less than a second.

"Shit, that's pretty good," he muttered to himself.

"Should be, based on the price you paid for it," Screech replied as he pushed the chair beneath a large dining table.

Drake raised an eyebrow.

"Do I want to know?"

Screech laughed his high-pitched titter.

"Nope. You don't want to know. It's better that way," he paused and chewed his lip. "You really think that we're going to get anything on camera?"

Drake shrugged, remembering the die-hard certainty in Greta Armatridge's voice the day prior.

"Maybe. I don't know. Doesn't matter, I guess. What matters is that Mrs. Armatridge keeps paying and we keep watching."

Screech nodded.

"Speaking of which, I'm getting hungry. How 'bout some breakfast? You're paying."

***

Drake's first instinct was to head to Patty's, but he changed his mind at the last moment. He hadn't been there since his final meeting with Ivan, and he was concerned that it would bring back memories that he would rather keep locked away.

The finger bone in his pocket was reminder enough.

Instead, he let Screech choose the breakfast joint.

The man didn't hesitate.

"Oh, yeah, I know the perfect place," he said with a smile.

An apparent fondness for pancakes, and to Drake's dismay, Screech chose a small, hole-in-the-wall cafe with a lineup that extended nearly all the way around the building. They only managed to get a seat because Screech was friendly with the owner—a massive, sweaty man with flour speckles coating nearly every inch of his body—who set them up at a makeshift table near the kitchen.

Drake took a seat, as did Screech, and the waiter was at their side immediately.

"Hey Screech, you want the usual?" the woman, who looked to be in her mid-fifties, asked between smacks of gum chewing.

"But of course, Linda. And my friend here..." he looked over at Drake. "You like pancakes? Shit, of course you do. Everyone likes pancakes. Get him an order of the special—a stack of blueberry with a side of bacon. That suit you right?"

"Sounds fine," Drake said with a shrug. "And a black coffee."

The woman nodded and started to turn, when Drake reached out and touched her arm gently.

"And a newspaper, if you have one."

"Sure thing," she replied, and then to the kitchen she yelled. "Mark, Screech wants the special, and his friend wants a stack of blue with a side of hog."

Drake cringed at the intensity of her voice. When he turned back to Screech, he was surprised to see him smiling.

"You know you can get the news on your phone."

"I know, but I'm a touchy feely kinda a guy."

Screech chuckled.

"So long as you don't get feely with me, I'm alright with that. And you're going to love this place, by the way. As your namesake says, *thank me later*."

Chapter 9

BECKETT WAS HALFWAY TO his car after leaving Suzan before his phone started to ring. Normally set on silent, when he heard the BAD BOYZ theme song filter up to him, he immediately answered it.

"Dr. Campbell," he said.

As usual, the voice that replied was curt, abrupt, and to the point.

"There is an apparent suicide at 529 3rd Ave, Manhattan."

Beckett's eyes shot up, and he glanced around. He was standing outside New York University Medical Center, and he was offered a clear view of the University and Tisch Hospital complex in the afternoon sky—bright, but also waning, like melting ice cream.

He could almost see 3rd Ave from where he stood.

"Say again? 3rd Avenue?"

"Correct. Apparent suicide. The ME's office said that you might be in the area, teaching a course at NYU. On scene officer reported it as cut and dry—a job for someone more junior—but if you are close."

Beckett hurried across the street, holding his hand out to slow several taxi cabs, and eventually made it to his car.

"I'll be there in ten," he said, popping the trunk and retrieving his black case. 3rd Ave was so close that it made more sense just to walk.

True to his word, Beckett arrived at the entrance of the high-rise apartment in under ten minutes.

The front door was open, and a single police car was parked out front, the lights flashing.

There was nothing out of the ordinary here; a suicide wouldn't call for any pomp and circumstance, and an ambulance clearly wasn't necessary.

And yet Beckett had a sinking feeling in the pit of his stomach.

Something's wrong here.

He had lost count of the number of crime scenes that he had been to during his tenure as a medical examiner, and he had seen some heinous things in his day, the least of which was a caterpillar jammed into a dead man's mouth.

Suicides? He had been to plenty of those, and now mostly deferred them to more junior colleagues. And yet... he couldn't shake the feeling that something *was* wrong here.

Beckett swallowed hard and approached the door. As he did, a uniformed officer was in the process of exiting, and he halted Beckett's forward progress.

"Dr. Campbell, ME," he said, holding up his black medical bag. The officer nodded and stepped aside.

"Fair warning: there's a hysterical friend of the deceased in there," the officer said, cringing dramatically.

As if on cue, a loud shriek followed him out of the apartment building.

Beckett tilted his head as if to say, *'welp, there she is,'* and then stepped through the door.

He entered the foyer, noting several dozen shoes on a plastic rack off to one side. There was a staircase off to one side leading to apartments on the upper floors, but it was clear that the one that Beckett was interested in was on the main floor. The sheer number of students outside the open apartment door was an indication that it was likely a shared home for university students, especially given the proximity to campus.

Beckett walked through this second door and immediately saw two officers struggling to lift a hysterical blond-haired woman off the middle of the floor.

"He didn't commit suicide! He wouldn't!" she cried in a shrill voice.

One of the officers sensed his presence and turned to face him.

ME, Beckett mouthed, and the police officer, a stern-faced man with a thin goatee, tilted his head to the left.

Beckett nodded and quickly moved in that direction, hurrying so as not to be observed by the sobbing woman. Looking around as he made his way down a narrow hallway, he noted no obvious signs of a struggle. Sure, the walls were dinged, and there were dozens of dark finger smudges along their length, but this didn't strike him as out of place in this house.

During his medical degree, and for half of his pathology residency, Beckett had lived with three other men. He wasn't ashamed to admit that they had been slobs. Incredibly busy slobs, but slobs nonetheless. They would let their mess and clutter build for an entire month. Then they would pool their money to hire a cleaning crew to come in and deal with it. They always made these arrangements over the phone, presenting themselves as responsible doctors who were just too darn busy saving lives to keep their abode clean.

This worked… for a while. The cleaning crews would come and do what they could with the place, but when Beckett or one of the other tenants called the following month, they would get the ring around. Eventually, they exhausted the phone book of cleaning services. Their saving grace was that Beckett had just started a rotation with the ME's office and spent half his time in the morgue. By sheer chance, he met a man several years his younger named Thomas Wilde, who was helping develop a process to obtain signatures from severely degraded DNA samples. At the time, Thomas was completing advanced degrees in both biochemistry and genetics, but he was also an entrepreneur. And one of his businesses just happened to be a crime scene clean-up company. Back then, Tom had been young and eager, and he had been keen to curry favor with Beckett and the ME's office.

In return for cleaning their apartment every month, Beckett would make sure to recommend him and his company for cleanup jobs after the ME cleared the scene. The two had quickly become friends—ironically, given how terrible the other cleaning services treated him—and to this day their friendship continued, while Tom's company grew to become the main crime scene cleanup crew for all of New York City.

This place wasn't as bad as Beckett's had been, but it was far from clean. Evidence would be difficult to discern from the refuse.

Evidence? This is a suicide, Beckett, not murder.

And yet the feeling in his gut that had first struck him in the entrance still ate away at him.

There's something wrong here.

The first room Beckett came to had a strip of yellow crime scene tape draped across the opening, but this wasn't what struck him first. That honor belonged to the smell, a mixture of stale piss and sour feces.

It reminded him of a backed up toilet.

Breathing through his mouth now, Beckett strode forward, ducking beneath the yellow tape.

The bedroom was dark, the sole window covered in a sheet that only allowed the fading afternoon sun to penetrate in gray wisps. The bed was unmade, and the cheap particle board desk off to one side was covered with several textbooks, half of which lay open.

A single ceiling tile lay broken on the carpet, causing Beckett to immediately look upward. In the gaping hole left by the missing tile, he spied a faded yellow rope wrapped around a water pipe buried in the ceiling.

The other end was wrapped around a man's neck.

The corpse hung in the gray light, his back to the doorway. His body was stiff, indicating that rigor mortis had set in, giving Beckett a rough time of death of anywhere between eight and twenty-four hours. The man was wearing a pair of jeans, the back of which were dark when his bladder and bowels had let go in death.

A fly buzzed somewhere in the corner of the room, drawn by the smell, which intensified as Beckett strode forward. The man was wearing his shoes, which Beckett thought strange, but not unheard of. After all, this was clearly the room of a student, a busy student at that, and busy students didn't often consider the condition of the carpet when a final exam loomed.

As he moved to the front of the corpse, Beckett continued to make mental notes. Starting at his shoes, untied he noted, his eyes slowly moved upward, observing the dark stain on the crotch, and the man's plain, and surprisingly clean, white t-shirt.

When his gaze fell on the man's face, he paid attention to the foam at the corners of his mouth, the dark purple bruising around his neck. The man's eyes were open and bulged slightly, petechial hemorrhaging giving him a concentrated freckle look that clearly didn't belong.

Only when Beckett took a step backward and appreciated the corpse's face as a whole, did he finally come to realize why he was so struck with a sense of unease.

A sound came out of his mouth then, something so foreign that he barely recognized it as of his own making.

After more than a decade practicing medicine, and half as long working for the ME's Office, Dr. Beckett Campbell audibly gasped at a crime scene for the very first time.

Chapter 10

"CAN YOU BELIEVE THIS fucking guy?" Damien grumbled as he scanned the newspaper.

"What?" Screech asked with a mouth full of pancakes. "Who're you talking about?"

Drake turned the paper around. Screech surveyed the front page, then went back to eating his pancakes.

"So what?"

Drake sipped his coffee and then turned the paper back around.

The headline, in big bold type, read: *Ken Smith has ten point lead in New York City Mayoral race.*

"So what? Seriously? This guy is a..." but Drake couldn't find the right word to finish his sentence.

What was Ken Smith, exactly?

Drake's initial inclination had been that the man was a monster, a heartless bastard driven by the only universal drive: power. But part of him refused to believe that; after all, he had been drunk that night when he had been invited into Ken's condo, and he could have easily misread him.

It wouldn't be the first time; hadn't he misread the Butterfly Killer so badly that it almost cost him another partner?

"He's what?" Screech asked. "A rich asshole? A pompous prick? A twisted bastard who's using his son's death to garner the sympathy vote?"

Drake's eyes darted up and again he was at a loss for words. Screech was turning out to be more astute than he had given him credit for.

This was *exactly* what Drake felt, deep down, buried beneath a comforter of his own shame, his own guilt and inadequacies.

Screech shrugged and took another bite of pancakes, dark blue syrup clinging to the corners of his lips.

"Yep, he's all of those things. But so what? Aren't all politicians?"

Drake thought about this for a moment before taking a bite of his own pancakes. Screech had been right; they were damn good.

And he was also right about Ken Smith.

He *was* all those things, but he was something else too.

Drake found his hand subconsciously moving to his pocket, his fingers wrapping around the hard finger bone within.

He was also a man of resources.

"You alright? I didn't mean to offend," said Screech.

Drake pulled his hand from his pocket, leaving the finger bone inside and shook his head.

It's not my problem anymore. I've said my piece, I've atoned for my sins. It's time to move on.

"Naw, it's fine—you're right. Good pancakes, by the way."

"The best," Screech said with a swallow. "Hey, let me ask you something… do you miss it?"

"Miss what?"

"Being a cop. I mean, I'm guessing that someone your age might get a kick out of watching Mrs. Armatridge's bedroom, but it has to pale in comparison to what you're used to, doesn't it?" Screech asked with a smirk.

The question caught Drake by surprise. He had hired Screech solely based on his technical skill set, his expertise with everything electronic. Long ago, back when he had been working the New York streets as a beat cop, Drake learned that the most common mistake in the field was that most people partnered up with others that were most similar to them. An ego trip if there ever was one; surrounding yourself with 'yes' men and bobbleheads. Sure it made you feel all warm and fuzzy inside, but this approach was a recipe for disaster. It was best to work with others that complemented your skills, not reinforced them, he knew. Clay, for instance, had been the cool, calm and collected yin to his yang. Level-headed. Able to deal with the likes of Sergeant Rhodes, whereas Drake just liked to bash heads.

Chase had been more like him, but she had a way of speaking to people, himself included, that made them comfortable enough to open up, without them even knowing.

And at Triple D Investigations, Screech was the computer wizard, someone who had the requisite know-how to set up teeny tiny cameras to record people's private lives. Drake had worked with Screech for the better part of six months now, and in all that time they hadn't so much as shared what their favorite color was, let alone anything intimate.

Which had suited Drake just fine.

Now, however, over a stack of delicious pancakes — Screech's favorite food, evidently — it was clear that the man was looking to open up.

Drake swallowed his pancakes and gnawed the inside of his lip.

"No," he lied, locking his eyes on Screech's.

The man raised an eyebrow.

"No?"

Drake felt as if the man was peering into him, and when he felt his face flush, it was he who finally looked away.

Why lie? What's the point of lying?

"Sometimes," he said in a small voice. "Sometimes I miss it. But that part of my life is behind me. It's about Triple D now, about carving out a small living for myself."

This answer seemed to satisfy Screech as he nodded, and went back to scarfing his pancakes. Drake did the same, but with slightly less enthusiasm than before.

For some reason, they suddenly tasted bland to him.

"He's going to win, you know," Screech said when his plate was finally clear.

Drake sipped his coffee.

"Who?"

Screech hooked a chin toward the paper that dangled over the edge of the small table.

"The lawyer. He's going to become the next mayor."

Drake's eyes darted to the image of Ken Smith, smiling a pearly-white smile, his hair so perfect that it was hard to imagine that is anything but fake.

Everything about the man looked fake.

"How do you know?"

Screech scoffed.

"You mean besides the ten-point lead?"

Drake grunted.

"Well, because he has the support of the police department, for one. And you probably know this better than most, but once a candidate has the support of the boys in blue, all the other dominoes will soon fall into place."

Drake's eyes scanned the photograph, trying to figure out where Screech had gotten his information from.

Is it common knowledge that Ken paid off the force? That Ken Smith had Sergeant Rhodes tucked so deep into his back pocket that he could smell the man's farts even before they left his ass?

He thought not—if anything, the NYPD liked to keep their inner workings to themselves. That is, unless a disgruntled and depressed detective decided to contact the Times about doing an exposé.

The photograph in the newspaper depicted a smiling Ken Smith, standing outside the library that Thomas had inaugurated only a few days before his death.

And there, at his side, was a man in a sport coat, his head turned back toward the building. The man was in profile, his face obscured by shadows, but Drake knew that Adam's apple anywhere, he recognized the harsh outline, could imagine it bobbing up and down like a whack-a-mole with every swallow. It was a lump that he had stared at for years.

It was Sergeant Rhodes.

Drake's eyes narrowed, and he turned back to face Screech, who was busy chomping on a slice of bacon that he had stolen from his tray.

The real question, he realized, was how Screech knew that this man was Sergeant Rhodes.

Chapter 11

H E WORKED SILENTLY, SLOWLY removing the unconscious man's clothes. The naked man was overweight, on the verge of morbidly obese, with pasty white skin and patches of dark hair that sporadically covered his chest and upper arms. Thankfully, he was already in the tub, for which the man wearing the black gloves was grateful.

He doubted if he would have been able to get him in there on his own.

Satisfied, the man leaned back and observed his victim, who was slumped in the cheap plastic tub, one fat arm overhanging the side, the other squished up against the tiled wall. His massive chest rose slowly, rhythmically, with every labored breath. His face was placid, his cheeks sagging. He observed the man, much as he had the others, for the briefest moment, watching and listening to the air wheeze out of his nose and mouth.

The fat man in the tub shuddered slightly, and this set the man in the gloves in motion. He leaned forward and grabbed the victim's pale hand. In it, he placed the large metal knife that he had taken from the kitchen. Then he wrapped his fingers over the other man's, squeezing the pudgy digits around the handle.

Without hesitation, he scraped the blade over the man's right wrist, moving from the base of his palm halfway to his elbow. The knife left a gray line in its wake, which remained dormant for nearly a full second. And then the blood started to ebb out of the slit, a slow trickle that soon became a steady stream.

The man stirred, and his eyelids fluttered. A moan left his mouth.

Releasing the victim's hand, he switched the knife to the other palm and repeated the process on his left wrist. When this wound started to pump blood, the man suddenly awoke.

"Wha—what's happening?" he blubbered.

Red streaks splashed the white tub and sprayed across the wall as he tried to force himself to a more erect seating position.

It was no use; he was too fat, and he had already lost too much blood.

For the briefest moment, their eyes met, and the man calmly crossed his gloved hands over his knee, once again observing the fat man.

"Sleep well, my friend. Sleep well, knowing that you served a worthy cause," he whispered as he watched the man die.

Chapter 12

BECKETT FUMBLED TO RETRIEVE his phone from his pocket. It was a near-impossible task; his fingers suddenly felt swollen, his sure-handed surgical prowess abandoning him.

He felt like a toddler trying to free his fingers from Chinese finger trap. Eventually, he managed to get his phone out, but now he had forgotten who he had intended to call.

A hand came down on his shoulder, and Beckett yelped, jumping away.

"Woah, Doc, you okay?"

Beckett whipped his head around to look at one of the uniformed officers he recognized from downstairs. The man was squinting at him suspiciously.

"We managed to finally get the girl out of the apartment—seems like she was a good friend of the deceased... claims it wasn't suicide. Says that the man wouldn't commit suicide, no way, no how," he hesitated. "Was it? Was it suicide?"

Beckett opened his mouth to say something, but no words came out. He simply stood there, trembling slightly, sweat forming on his forehead despite the cold air filtering up to him from the open door behind him.

The officer reached forward and went to put a hand on his shoulder again.

Beckett pulled back.

"Don't touch me," he managed to croak. The officer stared for a moment, confusion and then hurt forming on his young face. "Sorry. I'm just not feeling so well all of a sudden."

The officer's expression softened.

"That's alright. It's the weather, I bet. You know, wet hair and cool air and all that."

Beckett resisted the urge to chastise the man, to call him an idiot. No one got sick from cold air.

"Yeah, must be," he said instead. Then, with a deep breath, he turned back to the hanged man.

His name was Dr. Edison, Eddie, Larringer, and he was a student in Beckett's forensic pathology class. In fact, it dawned on Beckett that Eddie was the one who had been missing from the exam earlier in the day.

I guess this is as good a reason as any to miss a test, Beckett couldn't help but think. And then he felt sick to his stomach. Of all the horrific homicide scenes he had attended, of which there had been many, he had never once come across the body of someone that he knew.

"Well," the officer said softly. "Was it suicide?"

Beckett steeled himself and observed the body again, thinking about how Eddie had been slowing down as of late, his answers in class becoming more erratic. These were clear signs of stress, and his grades were suffering because of it. In fact, Beckett had already come to the conclusion that he would keep Eddie back a year, just to make sure that he was ready for the big leagues.

And now… *this*.

Looking up at Eddie, Beckett realized that there was something oddly familiar about the way he was hanging, about the way his eyes bulged and were surrounded by broken blood vessels.

He swallowed hard.

"Yeah," he said in a dry voice. "It certainly looks like a suicide. Let's bag his hands for evidence just in case and get him down, shall we?"

Chapter 13

TRY AS HE MIGHT, DRAKE couldn't shake the feeling that something was terribly wrong. And for some reason, he had the sneaking suspicion that it had something to do with the young doctor, Eddie Larringer.

After pancakes, he spent the rest of the day sipping on whiskey and watching the boring meanderings of Mrs. Armatridge and her husband, who, for the record, was confined to a wheelchair for ninety-percent of the day. This did little to help him ignore the nagging sensation in his gut.

This one is different; it's not the same person, not the same crime. It's been staged… he's been murdered.

Drake was sitting on the worn couch in his apartment, drink in hand, cell phone in the other. The TV was on in the background, but even if pressed he would've have had a hard time recounting what was on.

And then there was the finger bone on the glass table, lying like an abandoned pile of salt.

He watched as Mrs. Armatridge went to the kitchen, said something to herself, then reached for a large knife. The woman teased it from the block and held it up to the light. In her reflection, Drake caught sight of a small smile she had on her weathered face.

What's she doing? he wondered, thankful for the distraction.

A flicker of movement from the upper right quadrant caught his eye. The maid, a one Consuela Ortiz, was helping Mr. Armatridge rise out of bed. As she leaned forward, lowering her full breasts level with the man's face, she helped swing his legs over the side of the bed. Except that wasn't all she did; Drake could have sworn that he saw her small, tanned hand sweep over his lap.

This in itself wouldn't have seemed out of place—after all, she was helping the man into his wheelchair and incidental contact was to be expected—but it was her face that made Drake frown.

A smile, one that was just wide enough to reveal a flash of white teeth, fleetingly appeared on Consuela's young face.

His eyes flicked to Mrs. Armatridge, who was curiously running her finger along the blade of the knife as if testing the sharpness of the edge.

Drake took a sip of his drink and shook his head, silently admonishing himself for such morbid thoughts.

That's all in the past, Drake. This isn't a murder scene—you're done with those. You've moved on. Get a grip.

And then an idea struck him.

I should go out. Go to a bar. Meet someone. A woman, perhaps.

His eyes flicked to the bone on the desk, and for the first time since Ivan had placed the envelope on the table at Patty's Diner, he didn't feel the accompanying pang of guilt in its presence.

Drake shut off his phone, and put it on the table beside the bone and then stood. Stretching his back, he sighed, then made his way to his bedroom.

Yes, he thought with something akin to pleasure, *I should go out.*

He grabbed a clean V-neck t-shirt and a pair of dark jeans from the top drawer of his dresser and put them on.

Then, with a smile, he made his way to the front door, not even casting so much as a sidelong glance at his past life.

***

Barney's was a local pub adorned by stained glass windows out front and a long bar that stretched the length of the pub, crafted from what had once been a massive piece of driftwood, inside. There were more taps standing at attention above the bar than there were kegs, but there were still enough kegs to satisfy even those with very specific malted barley tastes. The bartender was a friendly man who had a decade on Drake—pushing closer to fifty than forty—with a severe look, but an air that suggested approachability.

Or at least, that was what Barney's *had* been three or four years ago when Drake and Clay had spent the occasional lazy afternoon inside its doors.

Now, however, Barney's was a completely different animal. For one, the massive wooden door had been replaced by two large gentlemen wearing black t-shirts that were two-sizes too small. In fact, there didn't appear to be an actual door at all. Behind these two men, Drake could see that the massive bar had been replaced by something sleek and black, and the worn leather booths Drake had become accustomed to had been usurped by waist-high tables made of some sort of reflective material. Barney's interior was dim, but as he squinted into the darkness, it was suddenly punctuated by bright flashes of light.

Drake knew that he was grimacing, but couldn't seem to scrape the expression from his face.

Barney's had gone from a majestic lion to some sort of autistic neon leopard.

Still, despite his apprehension, Drake took a step forward. As he did, the bouncers moved closer to each other, blocking the open doorway.

"Fuck this," Drake grumbled and turned, intent on heading back to his car and getting the hell away from this electric eyesore.

But a voice from within, which somehow managed to pierce the dull thud of dance music, hollered his name.

"Drake? That you? Jesus fucking Christ! Get your ass in here!"

Drake turned back and squinted hard, and as he did, the strobe lights flashed, and he caught sight of the bartender, of the man he knew as Mickey Roots. His severe expression was gone, and his narrow faced seemed to have filled out slightly, aided by the presence of a thick gray mustache.

"Hey Tweedle-Dee and Tweedle-Dum, let him in! Let Drake in!" Mickey shouted, waving an arm dramatically.

The bouncer's faces twisted into matching scowls, but they wordlessly parted to allow him passage.

And yet Drake hesitated. Part of him thought that this bar had become some sort of portal that would transport him to another dimension.

This wasn't him.

He was the *old* Barney, this was… this was like a title of an early Tom Wolfe novel.

But why was he clinging to the *old* Barney? The old Barney meant staying at home, staring at his cell phone, at the finger bone, thinking of Clay and Chase and times long past.

"Fuck this," he repeated, only this time, it felt good to say the words. Holding his head high for the first time in what felt like forever, he moved toward the open door. As he passed the bouncers, he said, "Why thank you, Tweedle-gentlemen."

Chapter 14

Beckett stumbled into his NYU office, breathing heavily. The image of Eddie's face, eyes bulging, foam at the corners of his mouth, was etched on his retinas, embossed on his mind.

He was so distraught that at first he didn't notice that Suzan was still sitting at his desk.

"Dr. Campbell?" she said softly, making him jump. He wiped the sweat from his brow and then brought his hand in front of his face, confused and worried that it was still trembling. "You alright? You don't look so well."

Beckett stared at her for a moment, unable to prevent himself from seeing her eyes widen, her tongue turn purple and swollen and hang from her heart-shaped mouth.

A shudder ran up his spine, and he had to physically shake his head to regain control of himself.

"I'm fine," he said, then bit the inside of his lip. "I'm not, actually. Hey, are you done correcting the exams?"

Suzan frowned.

"On the last one," she informed him. "But I really think that you should go over them just in case. Some of the answers…"

Beckett waved a hand dismissively.

"Don't care about the answers. Did you come across the exam for Eddie Larringer?" he asked, knowing the answer already.

Suzan looked down and flipped through the stack of exams.

"No, I don't think so."

Beckett felt his heart flutter in his chest.

"Did he skip the test?"

"Yes," he whispered. He began to think a little more about the events of the day, trying to piece together why things felt so strange, when this foreboding sensation initially begun.

Was it when at the cafe this morning, getting his usual coffee when the woman with the piercing blue eyes had bumped into him, spilling her latte on her cream-colored blouse? When she had cursed him as if he had done something wrong?

No, that wasn't it. That was a usual occurrence for New York.

Well then, what?

"Beckett? Do you want me to go? To let you sit? You still don't look well."

"No," he grumbled. "Just keep grading, please."

And then it hit him. The strange feeling had come over him when the PowerPoint images had started cycling.

It was the image of the man who had died from positional asphyxia that had set him on this course.

Beckett snapped his fingers, causing Suzan to startle.

Yes! That's it, the sweater was different!

"Beckett?"

Beckett walked over to her side of his desk.

"Scooch," he said, and she slid her chair to one side. Beckett reached down and opened the door to his desk.

Two days ago, someone had left a folder with images from the exam on his desk. At the time, he thought it was the Dean of Medicine, but he had been so busy he hadn't bothered to follow-up on it.

Only now, it wasn't there.

He rubbed his chin and squinted at the myriad of branded pens, stress balls, and USB drives adorned with one pharmaceutical name or another.

"Suze, can you pull up the images from the exam on the computer?"

Suzan nodded and started punching away at his computer. He had left it open and it didn't require a password... against school policy, of course, but he didn't much care for policy.

He cared about solving problems, mysteries, and for some reason, despite the obvious signs that Eddie had committed suicide, he was beginning to think that there was something deeper going on here.

Something insidious.

The PowerPoint started running and Beckett stared closely at the image on the screen. As expected, it depicted the man bent over on his own neck. The man in the striped sweater.

It is *different*, he concluded, remembering how the stripes had been vertical in the image that had been left on his desk, while these ran horizontally.

The image flicked over to the next image, this time of a hanged man. Suzan accidentally clicked the mouse and the next slide appeared, showing an obese man in a bathtub, his wrists slit.

"Wait! Go back!"

Suzan clicked again, and Beckett felt his blood run cold.

"No," he moaned, and for the second time this day, the second time in as long as he could remember, Beckett felt fear course through him.

This image was of a man hanging from the ceiling, a drop ceiling tile removed, one end of a faded rope wrapped around a water pipe, the other around his neck.

The man's back was to the photographer, but Beckett could clearly see that he was wearing dark jeans with a soiled spot between the two rear pockets. He was also sporting a clean white t-shirt and a pair of worn Converse sneakers, the laces untied.

"This is… impossible," he muttered, blinking rapidly, wondering if he was still somehow hungover, or if the Ayahuasca he had indulged in a couple of months back in Montreal was finally coming back to haunt him.

"What? What is it?" Suzan asked.

Beckett swallowed hard.

"I just… I just saw this man, hanging from the ceiling," he gasped. "This is Eddie Larringer."

Chapter 15

Drake fumbled to open the door to his apartment, while at the same time holding the back of the woman's head, their lips pressed together in a sloppy, drunken kiss.

He cursed when he dropped his keys. Peeling her off him, he bent to grab them. As he did, the woman thrust her hips forward seductively, moving her crotch, hidden behind her black satin dress, in his direction. Drake slid up her body, pressing his jeans against her, watching as her chin rose, a soft moan escaping her mouth. He kissed the corner of her jaw, then finally managed to open his door. He thrust it open, and then wrapped his arms around her thin waist, and picked her up and entered his apartment.

He used the heel of his shoe to slam the door closed behind them.

Then Drake started kissing her again, breathing in her scent, the lingering aftertaste of his own whiskey-laden breath mixed with the sweetness of the Prosecco that she had been drinking.

They barely made it to the couch. Drake had lifted the woman's dress over her head and was now kissing her on the neck, shoulders, every pale, perfect patch of skin that he could find. She was wearing a sexy black bra and lace panties beneath her dress, and in only a few seconds, he had removed those as well.

And then he too was naked. Drake lowered the woman onto the couch, the couch that he had spent many nights on alone, and then resumed kissing her, stroking her, and finally, entering her.

She gasped loudly and her hand flew out, knocking into the coffee table. Drake heard the sound of something falling off the table but paid it no heed.

It didn't last long. It was good, but it had been a while since Drake had been with a woman and it showed. And yet, she seemed satisfied. Breathing heavily, Drake pulled himself off of her and sat up, lifting his boxers to his waist.

The woman started to trace lines on his bare back.

"Mind if I smoke?" she asked gently.

Drake said he didn't mind, and then, at the last moment, added, "have one for me?"

He hadn't smoked for nearly as long as it had been since he had laid with a woman, but when she handed him a Belmont and he took his first drag, it was as if he had never quit. As he smoked he poured a drink from the bottle of Johnny Red, offering her one first.

She was pretty, with small, girlish features, and blond hair that feathered about her head. But it was her body that had first attracted him to her, from the very second he had stepped into Barney's.

Lithe, muscular, and pretty near perfect.

The only problem was, he couldn't remember her name.

She, on the other hand, remembered his well.

"Drake," she said absently as she took a drag of her cigarette. The smoke mixed with the glow from the burning cherry and gave her pretty face an almost ethereal appearance. "Like the rapper."

Drake nodded. This wasn't the first time he had heard this; in fact, Screech had gotten into the habit of calling him this exact thing-*Drake the rapper*—on several occasions.

"Yeah, but I'm the original," Drake said with a smirk. He took a sip of his drink, then took a drag of his cigarette.

He noticed the red light on his cell phone blinking and knew, thanks to Screech's tutelage, that he had a message waiting. Drake reached over and picked it up, swiping the bottom and punching in his code to unlock it.

He was wrong; there wasn't a message waiting—there were a half dozen, and they all came from the same number.

From Beckett.

Drake stared at the phone for several seconds.

"Everything all right, Drake?"

Drake scrolled to the text message section and read the first few messages.

Drake, need your help.

Drake, answer your damn phone.

Something fucked up is going on, need your advice.

You a fucking detective or what?

Drake?

DRAKE???

Without thinking, he clicked the button at the bottom, making the screen go dark.

Not my problem anymore, he thought, then turned back to the beautiful, naked woman on his couch, a smile on his face.

He gently teased the cigarette from between her fingers, watching her brow furrow in confusion. Then he dropped his own cigarette along with hers into his half-empty glass of scotch, extinguishing them both with a loud hiss.

"Nothing's wrong," he said as he leaned close to her again. "Nothing, except I think I should improve on my previous performance."

Drake pressed his lips against hers, relishing her surprise. When his fingers traced a line up the inside of her smooth thigh, her eyes slowly began to close and her breathing became ragged.

I'm done with that life—this is my life now.
He cupped her breast with his other hand.
And I think I'm going to like it.

Part II – Accidental

Chapter 16

CHASE ADAMS RUBBED HER eyes and watched as the scuba driver's head broke the surface of the water. He raised a thumb, and Chase felt a scowl form on her face.

"Get the lights up over there," she instructed a uniformed officer. The man nodded and started rearranging one of the large gray light fixtures.

Eventually, another diver appeared beside the first, and he too held up a thumb. This time they were awash in harsh light that reflected off the otherwise serene body of water.

"Bring the body up, then," Chase said to anyone who would listen. "Bring it up and lay it on the shore."

Then she shook her head and swore under her breath.

It was going to be a long night, meaning that she wouldn't see her husband or son going on six nights in a row now.

Chapter 17

BECKETT LOOKED OVER AT Suzan, who was combing through the stacks of files on his desk, looking for the folder of images containing what he had initially thought were for the forensic pathology final.

"Nothin'?" he asked.

Suzan looked up at him with tired eyes.

"No, can't find any photographs at all."

Beckett breathed deeply and closed his eyes. When Eddie's face floated across his vision, they snapped open again.

"Why don't you go home, Suze? Get some rest. Do you have class in the morning?"

"Yes, but not until ten. It's not even midnight yet, I can look a while longer."

Beckett considered this for a moment, then decided against it. If she hadn't found the folder now, then she wasn't going to find it at all.

It wasn't here—someone had come in and taken it.

But who? And why?

And why the fuck won't you answer your phone, Drake?

"It's not here," he said flatly. "But if you want to stick around, then I could probably use your help. You good at searching for things on the Internet?"

Suzan made a face.

"Of course—but that depends on what I'm looking for, I suppose."

Beckett chewed his lip. He wasn't even completely sure himself, and he was beginning to feel that maybe he had just imagined the comparisons between Eddie's hanged body and the image from the test. He had recused himself from the case and had sent one of the junior MEs to finish the report on

Eddie and to bring the body back and look for trace, but that didn't mean he couldn't check in later to make sure.

In fact, it would be irresponsible for him, as the acting Senior ME, not to review the results.

It *could* have been a coincidence, he decided. After all, how many suicides took place in NYC year on year? Two hundred? *Three* hundred? And how old were the images from the test? They weren't *his* images, but he thought he could remember seeing them when he had taken the forensic pathology final exam himself more than a decade ago.

So, it was possible... and yet, what were the odds of it happening to a young doctor about to take this very test? And if it wasn't a coincidence, what did it mean?

Did Eddie commit suicide in a way that mimicked the test itself? A way of punishing Beckett as a final, ironic goodbye? But if so, how did he obtain the images?

Beckett cleared his throat and decided to let Suzan in on what he had seen.

"Here's the thing, Suze. I just went to a crime scene, and one of my students apparently committed suicide," he pointed to the image of the man hanging on the screen. "It looks nearly exactly like this. I mean, almost exactly. Same shoes, same one tile missing. Same rope, same clothes."

He let this sink in for a moment. Beckett wasn't sure what he expected in terms of a response, but it wasn't this: just a blank stare.

"Okay," he continued, trying to stir up some emotion. "But there's something else. You know the positional asphyxia case?"

Suzan indicated that she did.

"Well someone put a folder of images on my desk a few days ago. The first image was of that scene, only it was just a little different. The sweater wasn't quite right."

Suzan leaned away from the computer, fingers poised above the keys.

"Were there other images in the folder?" she asked.

Beckett thought about this for a moment, before nodding.

"Yes, I think there was a stack of them. But I only looked at the first. I thought it was just a copy of the images from the test, something that a colleague had left on my desk, and shoved it in the drawer. I didn't even look at them all."

Suzan nodded and turned back to the computer. As she typed away, she said, "So you think that someone is murdering people and staging their deaths to look like accidents? Like the suicides in the test?"

Beckett smirked; despite everything, he couldn't help it.

That was *exactly* what he was thinking, only he hadn't been so bold as to say it out loud.

But he wasn't about to let her get off that easily.

"Maybe," he muttered. "Maybe."

Suzan continued to pound away at the keyboard and brought up a block of text. Her lips moved slightly as she read it to herself, then paraphrased for Beckett.

"You're the fifth professor of the course since it was officially renamed forensic pathology about thirty years ago," she stated matter-of-factly. "The course website doesn't give me much information about the exams, only that there will be a practical and written component. I think—wait a sec," Suzan suddenly leaned forward. She clicked on a link and the screen suddenly opened to a PowerPoint presentation. She clicked through several pages of notes, then the image of the man who had died from positional asphyxia flashed onscreen.

Beckett leaned in close.

"That's it. That's the image from the test."

"Yep. This is… uh, Dr. Tracey Moorfield's class notes. Apparently, she posted her notes online for students to look over at home."

She scrolled through several more images and notes, before stopping at the image of the man hanging from the ceiling.

Beckett cringed at the sight.

"So, this available online, to everyone?"

Suzan shook her head.

"No. Only to NYU students and staff. And look here—" she clicked again, and an error message came on screen, — "can't even download or create a screenshot."

Beckett stood straight and stretched his back.

"Thank you—at least that's something to go on. Now go home, Suze. Go to class tomorrow morning, and I'll see you in the afternoon. Around the same time?"

Suzan's eyes narrowed.

"Where are you going?"

Beckett broke into a smile.

"I'm going to see if I can't find Dr. Moorfield, ask her a few questions."

"Now? It's almost midnight."

Beckett winked at the girl.

"If she's still a professor, then she'll still be here. Trust me, I'll find her."

And then I'm going to find out where the hell Drake is, he almost said, but bit his tongue at the last moment.

Chapter 18

"ANYONE HEARD FROM THE ME yet? Is Beckett on his way?" Chase asked, staring down at the body. She pegged the deceased's age at anywhere between twenty and thirty years, although she had been submerged for so long that it was difficult to tell for certain.

The victim had black hair that clung to her scalp, and her gums were pulled back, revealing stark white teeth in a sadistic grin. She was still wearing her clothes—a leather jacket and matching pants—but the former was open, revealing a black swimsuit top, and the bottoms were pulled down, revealing a matching swimsuit bottom.

Her hands were probably the worst: the skin was wrinkled and had turned a pale, ghostly white. As soon as the scuba divers had pulled her out of the pond and had laid her on the reflective blanket for specimen and evidence collection, foam started to bubble at the corners of her mouth. Now, a three-inch-high froth extended from the orifice like some sort of horrific experiment.

Chase grimaced.

"Anyone?" she asked again.

A uniformed officer appeared at her side.

"I've tried calling the ME, but I'm not getting an answer. Want me to keep trying?"

Chase nodded.

"Try to reach anyone at the ME's office. I'll try Beckett directly. Nobody touch the body until I say so, got it?"

The half dozen people milling around the pond, passing in and out of the bright lights they had erected, grumbled agreement and then continued about their business.

Whatever the hell that was.

Chase took her cell phone out of her pocket and turned her back to the others. She scrolled through her list of contacts, noting with a pang of guilt that Drake's name was on the same screen as Beckett's.

I should reach out to him. After all, he saved my life.

Things had ended amicably enough between them, and although no one had told her directly, Chase suspected that Drake had fallen on the sword—*her* sword—for the mistakes they had made during their chase for the Butterfly Killer.

Triple D Investigations, she thought, remembering the name of the PI firm that she had found when Googling his name.

I should call him, go have drinks.

Then she remembered Drake's breath reeking of whiskey, of him hovering over Dr. Mark Kruk's fallen body, convinced that he was going to kill the man.

Alright, maybe not a drink. Pie, then?

Beckett's answering machine picked up, and Chase left a message.

"Beckett, it's Chase. We have a body here in a pond in Central Park. Looks like a drowning, a prostitute, probably, except…" she paused.

Except what?

Except something didn't seem right about it.

"We're going to check some of the cameras, but we need you to come clear the body. You or someone else from the ME's office. Give me a call when you get this. Chase."

Chase hung up and turned back to the body, crouching on her haunches. She tilted her head to one side, staring at her milky eyes, the foam that bubbled from her mouth.

What's your story? She wondered with a strange sort of abstraction. *How did you end up here?*

Chapter 19

DR. TRACEY MOORFIELD WAS old enough to be retired, but she wasn't. Like most doctors, she would work until either she was physically incapable of functioning, or the university kicked her out. But because Tracey had tenure, only the former was a possibility. And judging by the way she deftly worked the pen in her left hand, Beckett thought that this was also out of the question.

Beckett found the elderly doctor in her office, a small cubicle tucked away in the back of the faculty club. He was briefly reminded of the scene from Office Space, in which they forced poor Milton to work down in Storage B. He thought something like that might be going on here; with tenure, the university couldn't force her out, they could only make her as uncomfortable as possible.

Putting a warm smile on his face, Beckett knocked lightly on the half-open door.

"Dr. Moorfield?" he said softly.

"Yes?" the voice returned, old, but strong.

Beckett eased the door open another foot or so.

"Hi," he said as he took in the scene before him. Beckett had never been in the faculty club before, despite being part of the faculty; he just hadn't seen the need for it. In fact, he doubted that he would be welcome, even given his status. Covered in tattoos, spiked blond hair on his head, and a matter-of-fact way of speaking that often came across as rude, Beckett was a bit of an outcast among his peers.

But this didn't bother him.

What *did* bother him, however, was the general and pervasive attitude possessed by many of the curmudgeonly doctors of yesteryear: a holier-than-thou attitude, often directing the construction of the pedestal upon which the public was all too eager to place them atop. Most of the doctors he knew, especially those entrenched in academia, had a god complex that rivaled the Pope's in terms of grandiosity.

Beckett knew instantly that Dr. Moorfield fit this mold very, very well. Shit, it was probably made specifically for her. It was in the way that her gray hair was perfectly styled, coming down to just below her chin in a sort of bob, and the way her white blouse was immaculate, even at midnight in the remote recesses of a building that the janitor probably wouldn't have been able to navigate without GPS support.

Her presence alone seemed to fill the air with particles of ego like glittering dust motes.

"Yes?" she asked again, raising an inquisitive eyebrow.

Beckett's smile broadened.

"My name is Dr. Campbell," he said politely, trying to put himself on her level.

Alas, there was only room for one atop ye pedestal of gold.

"And? Do you need something?"

Beckett stepped into the room, catching her flinch slightly as he did. The woman tried to hide her discomfort, but he saw through her mask.

"I do, actually. I'm teaching the forensic pathology course and had a few questions for you."

The woman pressed her lips together tightly.

"I thought Dr. Jablonsky was teaching that class."

Beckett shook his head.

"He was, but not anymore. I took it over a *coupla* semesters ago. Look, I can see that you are busy," he said, half hoping that she picked up on his tongue and cheek comment, "but I just had a few questions for you—about your slides."

A look of confusion crossed over her face.

"What slides?"

"The ones from your course… the test review material? For the final?"

"Ah, yes. The written portion of the final. I always found that part of the course to be useless. Tried my best to get it removed. If the residents spent half as much time in front of bodies as they did at their computers, then maybe we would have some actual competent pathologists today."

Evidently, Beckett's dig hadn't gone over her head.

She had just lobbed it back at him.

Touché.

Beckett didn't say anything, and eventually, Dr. Moorfield sighed and laid her pencil on her desk. Then, with an action so deliberate that it was almost comical, she interlaced her wrinkled fingers and leaned forward.

"What about it, Dr. Camel?"

"Campbell," Beckett corrected.

"Pardon?"

He shook his head.

"Never mind. I just… I just wondered if you could take them down, off the website. I mean, I think they're great notes and all, but I feel like using the exact images from the prep exam as the actual exam is giving the students an unfair edge," he said, surprised at how easily the lie came to him.

When he had first called his friend in the Dean's Office and had inquired about Dr. Moorfield — waking him up from what sounded like a deep, satisfying slumber — he hadn't the forethought to come up with a story as to why he was inquiring about the notes.

Surely, he couldn't reveal his suspicions to this curmudgeon. So now he was flying by the seat of his pants.

And it was... oddly exhilarating.

"My notes are online? On the Internet?"

"Yep. On the class website. It's archived, but all you need is an NYU medicine email address and password and you can get in to view them."

The elderly doctor cleared her throat.

"I was unaware of this. I'll speak to the department, see if they can take them down in the morning. Lord knows, the last thing we need are immature, unqualified physicians that are getting hand fed the test answers, as well. Wouldn't you agree?"

Boom, another dig.

Beckett couldn't help but smirk. She was good. Old, crusty, but adroit.

"That would be great," he replied, but made no move to leave.

"Anything else?"

Beckett chewed his lip.

"Well, yeah, I guess. One more thing: did you take the photographs, personally? Like I said, we still use them today. I've been to my fair share of crime scenes—homicides, suicides, accidents—but have never been able to capture the poses and positions as accurately as the photographer of the test photos. I mean, geez, they must be, what? Fifteen years old? Twenty? And I'm still using them. That says a lot, given how cameras have evolved over time."

Dr. Moorfield stared at him for a good minute before replying. Beckett knew that she was sizing him up, trying to figure out if he was mocking her again, but he didn't break.

"I took them," she admitted at last. "And they're closer to twenty years old by now. Took them back during a time when becoming a doctor meant actually doing things—performing autopsies, surgeries, speaking to patients—instead of just reading about it. As for cameras, nothing has really changed. I mean, you can't click a button and put bunny ears or halos on a face with the Nikon I used back then, but that's about the only difference."

"Ah, well, I just wanted to say they are incredible pieces of art, really."

Dr. Moorfield scoffed at this.

"Medicine is not an art; it's a science, a discipline. You would do well to remember that, Dr. Camel."

"Of course, you're right. But still… they really are unique. Let me ask you something, did you ever think to put them in an exhibit of sorts? Copyrighting them?"

"An exhibit? No, Dr. Camel, it never crossed my mind. They are a surrogate for real learning, that's it."

Beckett struggled with the phrasing of his next question. Unlike his previous lies, she really hadn't given him an avenue to continue the conversation with the last one.

"Well, if it were me, I would be worried that someone would take them off the NYU server and sell them. I mean, you can get photos of nearly anything online, but those photos? They might fetch a pretty penny."

Dr. Moorfield fought a scowl and lost.

"I'm not interested in the money," she said bluntly.

Beckett held up his hands defensively.

"Yes, of course not. I wasn't thinking about you. I was thinking about others who might be inclined to steal them. I mean, once you take them off the website, there might still be other copies floating around somewhere. Any idea who might have copies?"

"You mean aside from Internet pirates?"

"Sure. There's no stopping them, anyway."

Dr. Moorfield thought about this for a moment.

"The police, I guess. They are, after all, from official crime scenes. Other than that, nobody. I don't even have the originals anymore. Had a fire a while back."

Something happened to her voice when she said the word fire; not quite a hitch, but a flash of anger, maybe?

Beckett locked this away for future reference.

"And you didn't put a folder on my desk? A couple of days ago?"

"Excuse me?" Dr. Moorfield asked.

He shook his head.

"Never mind. Thank you," he said.

Dr. Moorfield made a *hmph* sound then unlaced her fingers and picked up her pencil. Turning her attention to the papers in front of her, she said, "If that will be all, Dr. Camel, then please, I have plenty of work to get through tonight."

Beckett chuckled.

"I'm sure you do," he said, and then left the room.

What an odd and vile woman, Beckett thought. He was about to add more choice words to his description when his phone buzzed in his pocket.

Walking briskly down the hall and out of earshot of Dr. Moorfield's open door, he answered it.

"Dr. Campbell."

"Beckett? It's Chase."

Beckett's throat suddenly felt very dry.

"Yes?" he croaked.

"Need you down in Central Park. Have a drowned Jane Doe I need you to release."

Chapter 20

"IT'S CALLED A FOAM cone," Beckett said in a quiet voice. His heart was racing, sweat beaded on his forehead despite the fact that he was under-dressed for the chilly September night.

"A what?" Chase asked, leaning down toward the drowned girl's mouth.

Beckett swallowed hard.

The crime scene in Central Park was just like photograph four from Dr. Moorfield's series. There were some differences—the light had been more diffuse in the original image, but, he thought, if he were so inclined, he might be able to adjust the lights to get something that was nearly identical.

"It's a foam cone," he repeated. "Happens with drowning: a mixture of surfactant, blood, water, and air from the lungs that emerges after a body surfaces."

"Is it... normal?" Chase asked.

Beckett turned and looked up at her, his shock at finding another victim that matched the forensic pathology exam momentarily forgotten.

"*Normal?*"

Chase grimaced.

"You know what I mean."

Beckett turned back to the body.

"Normal for drowning, sure," he grabbed her arm and turned it over. He was going to look for track marks on the woman's arms, when he noticed her hands and stopped cold.

It was another photograph from the exam.

"Washerwoman hands," he whispered. This was too much. Too much to be a coincidence.

He had to tell Chase.

"What?"

Beckett looked around and was surprised by the number of people that were crowded over the body. There must have been six or seven officers, some of which seemed to be taking longhand notes of all things.

Their conversation would have to wait.

"The skin gets super wrinkled, starts slipping. Happens when a body is submerged for a few days," he said. To prove his point, he used the index finger of his gloved hand to push the flesh on the woman's palm back and forth. It moved freely and much further than what would be normal in a living human. Satisfied, he lifted the girl's leather jacket, revealing several track marks on the inside of her elbow.

"Some of these are recent," he informed Chase and the other officers.

"Suicide?" Chase asked. "Accident?"

Beckett had to bite his tongue.

Under any other circumstances, he would have said accident. Partial overdose, followed by a poor decision to either go swimming or simply falling into the water.

But that was before the others.

Beckett settled for, "Probably accidental. Will know more once we get her back to the morgue, do a couple of tests."

Chase, apparently satisfied, clapped her hands.

"Okay, let's wrap this up, people. Bullock and Noons, stick around with the crime scene until morning. Once I call you, after Dr. Campbell confirms that this was an accident, you can call Thomas Wilde to come clean it up. Everyone else, please help pack Jane Doe into the van and go home."

The group of detectives and officers started to move, and Chase leaned close to him.

"You alright, Beckett? You seem... *off.*"

Beckett rose to his feet.

"I—there's something I need to talk to you about," he looked around. "In private."

Her eyes narrowed.

"Sure. My office, or yours?"

"Mine. But not today. Tomorrow, maybe. But I won't clear the body until after we chat."

This seemed to annoy Chase, which clearly showed on her face.

"Please," Beckett continued. "It's important."

Although still not impressed, she nodded.

"Sounds good. I'll see you at your office at nine."

Beckett shook his head.

"No, not my office—not the ME office, anyway. My office in the university. I'll text you the room number."

"Fine. Now I'm going to get some sleep. Sorry to have dragged you out here so late."

With that, she turned and started to walk away, when something occurred to Beckett.

"Hey, Chase?"

She turned.

"Yeah?"

"Did someone take pictures of the scene?"

"Yeah—Officer Noons did. Took pictures just as you instructed."

Beckett nodded, remembering how he had told the burly man to take several pictures before he had started pointing out the details on the corpse to Chase.

"Yeah, but before that—before I got here. A police crime scene guy? CSU?"

"Yes. I think he was CSU. Took some photographs of the body being removed, of the hands, the face. Common practice. Why?"

"No reason. But I would like to speak to him. Have a project idea. You know what his name is?"

Chase pressed her lips together and shook her head.

"No clue. I'll find out, though. That all?"

Beckett forced a smile.

"That's it. Go get some sleep."

Chase frowned.

"Yeah, like I'm going to get any sleep after learning about washerwoman hands and foam cone," she replied.

Chapter 21

IT WAS CLICHÉD, IT was annoying, but damn it felt good.

Damien Drake was actually whistling as he strode toward his small office in the plain, Medical Arts building.

Whistling, and smiling broadly.

Last night had been good... no, it had been *great*.

And the woman—who he had later deftly determined was named Alyssa—she had been even better.

Drake sipped on his coffee as he walked up the first flight of stairs—he couldn't remember the last time he had taken the stairs when there was a fully functioning elevator—and when he made it to the door emblazoned with the words *Triple D Investigations*, he was surprised to find it unlocked.

He pushed the door open.

"Hello?"

Screech, who in addition to being Triple D's techno-wizard also acted as the secretary, was sitting in his chair, a pair of earbuds jammed in his ears. He didn't look up when Drake entered.

"Screech, take the fu—"

Drake caught himself before cursing.

Screech wasn't the only person in the office, he realized. The four chairs that they had optimistically pushed off to the right—worn burgundy things that they had scavenged from the dental office below them that was undergoing renovations—were filled. Not only that, but there was a woman in a walker leaning awkwardly against the wall.

Drake tried to disguise his shock with a smile.

He never took the stairs, and these chairs were never full.

"Good morning," he said.

Three of the four women, who were all gray-haired soup slurpers, raised their heads and returned the greeting. The fourth appeared to be sleeping.

What the hell are they doing here on a Sunday? On any *day?* He wondered.

"I'll be right with you," he said, still smiling. He strode over to Screech and yanked the earbuds out by the cord. The man yelped, then his eyes widened when he saw it was Drake.

"Hey Screech, can you by any chance see me in my office for a minute? Please, if you aren't busy, of course."

***

"What in the *fuck* are they doing here?" Drake asked in a hushed tone once the office door was shut behind them.

Screech's eyes bulged.

"How the hell should I know? My guess is that Mrs. Armatridge told her bridge buddies about us."

Drake stared at his partner for a long while, trying to get a glimpse into the inner workings of his brain.

"What?" the man said, recoiling slightly. "You're looking at me like I got two heads."

Drake ignored him.

"Mrs. Armatridge? Really?"

He was picturing the woman with her pearls, and then the strange expression on her face as she pulled the knife from the cutting block.

But then his mind flicked to the check worth ten grand that he had already cashed.

Drake pushed his lips together and rocked his head back and forth.

"Well shit, what are we waiting for? Let's get them in here and see what we can do for them," he said with a grin.

Screech nodded, turned, and walked toward the door, a spring in his step. His hand grabbed the doorknob, but before turning it he paused.

"Wait a second... wait just a *seeeeeecond.*"

Screech turned to face him, a sly expression on his face.

"What?"

"Why you so happy? You come in here, whistling, clicking your high heels together like Dorothy on speed. What gives?"

Drake went to his desk and sat. Instead of answering, he concentrated on shuffling papers aimlessly across the worn surface.

"You fucking sly dog," Screech said with a chuckle. "You boned last night, didn't you?" he looked toward the door, peering through the frosted glass at the hunched shapes in the reception area, then turned back to Drake and leaned toward him. "You got your tip wet, didn't you?"

Drake laughed; he couldn't help it.

Tip wet... sick.

"Shut up, Screech. Just keep your mouth shut and let's make us some money."

***

It was nearly noon by the time the last of the octogenarians scuttled out of Triple D like some sort of clutter of spiders. Drake was tired, tired of placating old women, of speaking in a louder than average voice, of repeating the same thing over and over again.

But despite his minor hangover and major annoyance, the smile on his face remained. It would take a lot more than this to make it go away, he realized. When they were finally gone and he was alone with his thoughts, he even resisted the urge to pour himself a drink.

"Screech! Get in here!" he hollered.

A moment later, the door opened and Screech's narrow face appeared in the gap.

"Yes, Leisure Suit Larry?"

Drake made a face. Screech's references were slowly degenerating into something reminiscent of Chase's. Obscure pop-culture nonsense that always flew over his head.

Drake took his time in answering, and the impatient Screech rolled his eyes.

"What is it, boss?"

"Come on in, sit down."

"Okaaaay," Screech said, doing as he was bid. "What's up?"

Drake let the man suffer a little while longer, but soon the charade was even starting to get on his own nerves. He reached into the top drawer of his desk, grabbed the four checks and threw them down.

"Seriously?" Screech tittered and grabbed the checks, eyes widening as he looked at them individually. "You closed every one of them?"

Drake held up his hands and forced a smug expression on his face.

"What can I say? The going rate has been set."

Screech laughed again.

"Well, I'd say that forty grand deserves a drink to celebrate, don't you?"

Drake shrugged.

"Yeah, sure, what the fuck."

Chapter 22

SUZAN WAS BACK IN Beckett's office when he arrived at work the next day, but this time, he wasn't surprised by her presence.

"Morning, Suze."

Suzan was busy typing away at his keyboard and looked up at him when he spoke. Her eyes were red, bleary.

"Jesus! When did you get here?"

She shook her head.

"I never left."

Beckett gawked.

"You *what*?"

"I never left," she repeated.

Beckett eyed her suspiciously, then glanced down at the coffee in his hand.

"Alright then," he said with a nod. "Drink this."

Suzan took the coffee cup from him and sniffed it. Her upper lip curled while at the same time the corners pulled downward.

"What is it?"

"Cold-brewed espresso, with a little *je ne sais quoi*."

Suzan raised an eyebrow, but didn't so much as hesitate before taking a slip. She swallowed, grimaced, and a second later had to cover her mouth with the back of her hand to stifle a cough.

Beckett laughed.

"That good, huh? So, all nighter? Been there, done that. Problem is, I have a sneaking suspicion that you haven't been spending your time studying, have you?"

Suzan ignored the question.

"Come over here, I did some more digging and I think I've found something."

Beckett hurried over to her side of the desk and peered at the computer screen. He had expected an image, another dead body perhaps, but was disappointed when he only saw a block of text.

"Yeah? What is it?"

Suzan cleared her throat and started to read.

"A police report on the body of an obese man in his forties found in his empty bathtub, wrists slashed with a kitchen knife. The ME ruled the death a suicide. That's the gist of it."

Beckett shrugged.

"So?"

Suzan turned and looked at him, a queer expression on her face.

"So?" she asked. Without waiting for an answer, she switched the screen to the PowerPoint presentation from the final exam. It was a close-up of three ragged gashes, deep enough to reveal red tendons and ligaments that looked like guitar strings, marking thick, pale wrists. Blood speckled the red bathroom tiles in the background. "So, there are no pictures in the police report, but this sounds the same, doesn't it? Fat man in tub, wrists slashed?"

Beckett was about to say that this could be anyone, but then bit his tongue. Fool me once, and all that. Instead, he offered, "When was the police report?"

Suzan switched back to the other screen and she moved her mouse pointer in a small circle around a date.

"The fourteenth... what was that? Ten days ago?"

"Eleven," Beckett corrected. He took a deep breath before continuing. "We have positional asphyxia, date unknown — I'm still trying to find the poor schlep in the system — then this guy, if he's related, then—" his voice hitched, "—Eddie's hanging. And last night I was called to a drowning in Central Park... the woman must have been submerged for some time. She had a foam cone and washerwoman hands."

Suzan made a strange, tight sound with her lips.

"Four bodies, all staged?"

"Maybe... maybe. Like I said, I'm still looking for the asphyxia case... I never signed off on it, must have been one of the junior MEs, but the body might still be around for me to look over. If not, there should be crime scene pictures somewhere," his mind quickly turned to the photographs that had been left on his desk.

Yeah, there are definitely photos of that case somewhere.

"It's a stretch, but... it seems almost impossible that these are all a coincidence, given how close together they are all. Which begs the question: what's next?"

Suzan frowned.

"Self-inflicted gunshot wound to the cheek, blowing out the top of the man's head. Then after that, there are three more. Eight in total. At least, that's what you have in your test."

Suzan's choice of words confused Beckett.

"What do you mean, *my* test?"

Suzan's face went dark and she pulled up another document on the computer. Beckett recognized it as Moorfield's test prep notes.

"Shit. That's still up? I told the witch doctor to instruct the department to take it down."

"Oh, it's down."

Beckett's eyebrows narrowed.

"I thought you said—"

"Meh, there are always workarounds. Anyways, I managed to override the screen capture block and took an image of each one of the slides."

"And?"

"And back when Moorfield ran the course, apparently there were some additional slides. I think that this information has since been switched to another course, because I can't find it in your syllabus.

Beckett felt his heart start to beat more rapidly in his chest, his mind racing as he tried to figure out what was left to teach in the forensic pathology course.

And then it came to him.

"Jesus, not *that*," he whispered.

Suzan didn't answer. Instead, she turned back to the computer and scrolled to the last test slide. Then she clicked once more.

Beckett's heart took a nosedive into the pit of his stomach.

Jesus Christ. Babies?

Chapter 23

THE MAN SAT IN his car with the engine off. It was midday, and he was parked under the shade of a large Oak tree. Cool as the air was, the sun was still bright and powerful.

It was the perfect vantage point.

No one saw him. And even if someone had noticed him, what could they say? A man, trying to hide in the shadows, trying to remain unseen.

And so what?

Most men cruising for prostitutes did this very thing. Especially here. Being discrete was the name of the game.

The man watched as several women—thin, gaunt things with sparse hair and sores on their lips—strolled by. A few of them glanced briefly over in his direction, but they never approached his car. Something kept them away, and he was glad.

After all, he wasn't looking for them. He was looking for something else, something more specific.

The man waited. And waited.

He was patient. He could wait a long time for what he needed, for the perfect specimen.

If his time in prison had taught him one thing, it was that waiting—watching and waiting—was a virtue that could not be overlooked.

But, as with the others, his patience wasn't tested; he didn't have to wait long.

A man with short red hair and chest hair of the same shade poking out the top of a sequined muscle shirt knocked gently on his window.

"Hey," the red-head said through the glass. "I seen you looking at the girls. Not interested in them, huh? Maybe you want something... different?"

He smiled when he said this, a valiant, yet failed effort at coquettishness.

The man rolled down the window a few inches and offered his own wry smile.

"You know what? I think you might be right. Why don't you hop in?"

Chapter 24

CHASE STARED AT THE images that Beckett had printed and laid on the table in his office.

Eight images, all depicting gruesome deaths, all of them suicide or accidental. The fourth looked uncannily like the Jane Doe they had just pulled from the pond in Central Park last night.

And yet, she still wasn't sure that she understood exactly what Beckett was telling her.

"So all of these are—what? Part of a test?"

Beckett nodded.

"Exactly. Part of the final exam for residents in forensic pathology. But, here—" he tapped the photograph of the drowned woman with the foam cone, then the image of her soft, wrinkled hands. "This is almost exactly the same as the woman we drudged out of the pond last night."

Chase tilted her head to one side, then the other as she observed the photo. It really did look similar. And yet, she remained unconvinced.

"Yeah, but so what? You said yourself that these photographs are meant to be representative. The fact that a body drowned in water for three days looks like this... isn't that to be expected?"

Beckett nodded.

"Sure, *representative*, but this is insanely close. *Too* close to be a coincidence. Maybe on its own I could chalk it up to coincide, but not when you take it with the others. Chase, look at me."

Chase's eyes flicked up and she focused on Beckett's. Six months ago, he had been a stranger to her, but ever since Drake had left the force, they had gotten closer. So close that she considered the man a good, if strange, friend and not just a colleague.

And she knew that he was serious about this, something that seemed out of place and inconsistent with his usual, jovial, sarcastic demeanor.

"I went to this crime scene, Chase," he said, tapping the photo of the hanged man. "I saw Dr. Larringer's body. This is no fucking coincidence. This is... this is *murder*."

Chase swallowed hard as she leaned over the table and indicated the second image, the one with the bloody wrists.

"And I went to this crime scene," she said softly. "I saw this man—Martin Dean. His death was ruled a suicide."

Beckett took a deep breath before responding.

"And the first one? Positional asphyxia? You ever seen something like this?"

Chase shook her head.

"Well I have," Beckett continued. "But not in person; in a photograph."

Chase once again raised her eyes to look at him.

"What do you mean? You've seen this picture?"

Beckett shook his head.

"No, not this one. But one almost exactly like it. Just..." he thought back to the lines on the man's sweater, how they went east/west. "But his sweater was a little different."

"You still have it?"

"No. Not anymore. I had it—I had a folder full of images—but it's gone. I think... I think someone stole it."

Chase grunted.

"What?"

Beckett sighed, and she sensed his embarrassment in this exasperated gesture.

"It was stolen."

"How—" but Chase didn't get to finish her question. The door behind her suddenly opened, and she spun around, her hand immediately going to the gun on her hip.

When she saw who it was, her hand fell away.

"What the—what the hell are you doing here?" she gasped.

Chapter 25

O**NE DRINK LED TO** another, as they always seem to, and before long, Drake found himself back at Barney's. He nodded to Tweedle-dee and Tweedle-dum, and the two large men reluctantly parted for him to enter.

"Mickey!" he shouted. The bartender smiled at him from behind the bar.

"Drake! Welcome back. I guess this place ain't half bad, after all."

Drake laughed.

"Guess not. Hit me up with a double of Johnny. Neat," he said as he took a seat at the closest end of the bar.

"You got it," Mickey replied.

As he waited for his drink, Drake glanced around. When he had come to Barney's the previous night, he had considered it a nightclub only—sorry, a *supper club*, as Mickey referred to it—but now, long before the sun had set, he realized that his assessment had been wrong in many respects. For one, it really wasn't that bad. Drake figured that with a few more drinks and by squinting his eyes, he might actually be able to imagine it the way it used to be.

Minus the driftwood bar, of course. While he would never love this iteration of Barney's, maybe, just maybe, he could get used to it. In fact, Drake was beginning to understand that a man could become accustomed to many things.

Like the death of their partner, say, or a complete change in careers.

He shook the thoughts from his head.

"Hey Mickey, you distilling my drink or pouring it?"

Again, the bartender laughed, and then quickly turned around, glass in hand. He slid it over to Drake, who finished half of it in one gulp.

"So, Drake, you have a good time last night?"

Drake swirled the remaining golden liquid in his glass, his memories turning to the way Alyssa had looked on his couch, the cigarette clutched between her full lips, her naked body glistening with a mixture of sweat and ecstasy.

"Yeah," he said softly. "As much as it pains me to admit it, considering I spent the evening in this eyesore, I guess I did. You seen Alyssa today?"

Mickey squinted at him while he twirled the corners of his mustache.

"Alyssa, hmm? She caught your fancy, didn't she?"

Drake shrugged.

"Maybe she did. Have you seen her?"

Mickey shook his head and turned his back to Drake. As he began preparing drinks for a couple who had sat at the other end of the bar, he said, "No, haven't seen her. Maybe she's working somewhere else tonight. Stick around, though, she might show up."

Drake opened his mouth to answer, but hushed whispers from the newly seated couple drew his attention.

He hadn't caught all of what was said, but two words were unmistakable: *Butterfly Killer*.

Drink in hand, Drake swiveled to face them, his lip curled upward in a sneer.

"Yeah? What about him?" he asked gruffly.

The man, who was thick through the chest and arms, with dirty blond hair tied up into a small bun atop his head, shot his girlfriend a weary look. The woman, who looked skinny enough to be a model, but not nearly unique enough, pursed her lips.

They both shrugged.

"You're that guy, aren't you?" the man asked.

"*That* guy?"

"Sure, the detective… uh, uh, the detective with the rapper name. Khalifa?" he snapped his fingers several times, trying to remember. "Naw. Lamar? Wheezy?"

This game was starting to annoy Drake, and he let his displeasure show on his face.

"Woah, sorry, bro," then the man's face lit up. "Drake! That's it, Detective Drake!"

Drake thought about coming back with something witty, snide maybe, or perhaps even intimidating, but he was too drunk to come up with anything on the spot. Besides, he was in no mood for an altercation. Taking another sip of whiskey, he held his free hand out to one side.

"Guilty as charged."

"Shit! Well, I'll be damned. You took that killer out, didn't you? Merked him good. I mean, that guy was ruthless, growing butterflies in those rich bastards' bodies like that. You're one bad mofo, ain't you, Drake?" Manbun looked as if he was going to say more, but his girlfriend elbowed him hard in the ribs, then whispered something in his ear that Drake didn't pick up.

"All of them?" the man asked. His girlfriend nodded emphatically. Manbun turned back to Drake.

"Well, looks like it's your lucky day. My girl here thinks that you're some sort of celebrity, wants me to buy your drinks tonight? What do you say, Drake? That sound good to you? A sort of thank you for taking that prick out?"

Drake smirked.

"What do I say? I say I hope you have a thick wallet, *bro*."

The smile slid off Manbun's face, and Drake immediately turned to Mickey. He was surprised to see that the bartender was standing directly in front of him, already holding up the bottle of Johnny Red. He was smiling so hard that you could see his top teeth despite the bushy gray mustache.

"Fill 'er up, barkeep. And keep 'em coming all night long… *bro*."

Chapter 26

"Shit," Beckett said. "Suze, I told you to come back *after* lunch."

Suzan Cuthbert stood in the doorway, a brown paper bag in each hand. She held them out to her sides, her eyes darting from Chase to Beckett and back again.

"I thought you might be hungry," she said innocently. "Who are you, by the way?"

Beckett watched as Chase's face contorted.

He spared her the introduction.

"Suze, this is Detective Chase Adams. She used to—"

Suzan's mouth instantly twisted into a grimace.

"You used to work with *him*, didn't you?"

Chase took a small step backward.

"Look, I know that—"

"—you don't know shit," Suzan spat. "That bastard… he got my dad killed. He fucked up and it cost me nearly everything."

The brown bags fell to the floor in an audible plop.

"Suze, I know how you feel about Drake—I do," Beckett said. "And I'm not going to try to convince you differently, but c'mon now. Be reasonable. Chase didn't choose her partner. Don't take your anger and hatred for Drake out on her."

Suzan's stern glare faltered for a moment, and Beckett continued quickly, seizing this moment of weakness to appeal to her morality.

"We have to work together to figure this thing out. We need Chase's help; we need her to stop a killer."

This seemed to do it; Suzan bent at the waist and picked up the bags. Then, with a heavy sigh, she said, "Well let's get at it then. I think I got enough for all three of us."

***

After wolfing down the greasy burgers—Beckett felt as if he hadn't eaten in a month—the three of them turned their attention to the photographs on the desk. As they looked them over, Beckett briefly went over his conversation with Dr. Tracey Moorfield, and then turned to Chase.

"I'm going to head to the morgue, see if I can find anything on the bodies, any evidence to suggest that their deaths weren't accidental or suicide. Chase, is there anything you can do back at the precinct, set up a task force maybe to find this guy? Like you did for the Butterfly Killer?"

Chase ground her teeth.

"That's going to be tough."

It was Suzan who spoke up next.

"Tough? We have a serial killer on the loose—a man who is making all of his murders look like suicide. Isn't that enough? I mean, this guy could have killed dozens of people already. How many suicides in New York City last year alone?"

Chase's reply was immediate.

"Over five hundred."

Beckett gaped.

"*Five hundred?* That has to be over a few years."

Chase shook her head.

"Last year alone. Closer to six hundred, actually."

Silence fell over them. Beckett's mind was struggling to wrap itself around the idea that over five hundred people committed suicide last year in New York City. He could personally remember a dozen or so that he had overseen, and while he knew that the ME wasn't called in for all cases of obvious suicide, he couldn't fathom the number being so high.

Suzan cleared her throat.

"Let's just focus on these ones for now," she said softly. Clearly, she hadn't expected the number to be that high, either. "So why can't we set up a task force?"

"Sergeant Rhodes... it's close to election time. He won't go on a wild goose chase, work NYC into a frenzy with another serial killer less than six months removed from the last one. I can't bring this to him, not like this. He won't go for this, no way, no how. Not without any evidence."

Beckett frowned. Although his interactions with Sergeant Rhodes had been limited, he had heard enough from Drake to know what an asshole he was.

"Like I said, I'll recheck all the bodies to see if I can find any evidence of foul play. But I'll tell you now, it's going to be tough. Two of the bodies have already been cleared."

His response, as rational as it was, seemed to enrage Suzan. This was just a little too close to home for her after what had happened to her father at the hands of the Skeleton King.

"So, what? We just wait for this guy to strike again? Really? That's the plan? Are we going to wait for the babies to die before we actually do something about it?"

Chase's eyes went wide and she turned to Beckett.

"Babies? What does she mean, babies?"

Beckett rubbed the bridge of his nose, closing his eyes as he did.

"There are eight images on the test, Chase, but—"

Beckett was interrupted by Chase's phone ringing. He opened his eyes as she turned her back to them and answered.

"Adams," she said, then listened. As Beckett watched, her shoulders started to sag. By the time she sounded off, her entire body seemed to melt.

She turned slowly, her eyes downcast. When she spoke, her words were barely a whisper.

"Looks like we won't have to wait long," she said, and then raised her eyes to look at the fifth photograph. "There's been another suicide."

Chapter 27

DRAKE STUMBLED OUT OF Barney's just as the sun started to dip below the horizon. His stomach was so full of whiskey that he could literally hear it sloshing in his belly with every step, and it seemed to set him off balance. As a result, he stumbled into one of the bouncers on the way out.

"Sorry," he grumbled, which came out more in a series of s's instead of an actual word.

Despite what Mickey had said, Alyssa had never showed, which had put him somewhat of a sour mood. Not completely sour, mind you; he still had a desk full of ten thousand dollar checks, a suddenly booming PI business, and a woman... somewhere.

Drake mumbled to himself as he sauntered onto the sidewalk. The line-up outside Barney's was starting to grow, he noticed, but this was mostly just for show. He'd been inside and it had been practically empty. Tweedle-dee and his partner -dum were just keeping people outside to make the bar look like it was more popular than it actually was.

Not a bad strategy, he surmised.

He blinked slowly and then continued down the sidewalk. Out of the corner of his eye, he saw a police car cruise by. It slowed, and Drake craned his neck to look at it.

Even through blurred vision, he thought he recognized the officer in the passenger seat. They locked eyes for a moment, and both Drake and the car came to a full stop.

The smirk sloughed off Drake's face.

"What?" he snapped. "What do you want?"

The officer, whose name escaped Drake, but whose face did not, frowned, then he rolled down the window.

Drake strode forward, unconsciously balling his fists.

"What?" he said again, louder this time.

The police officer hawked, then spat a loogie on the ground just beside Drake's shoe. Drake charged toward the car, raising his fists in front of him. But before he made it to the car, the officer rolled up the window and sped off. Drake reached for the bumper, but his depth perception and balance were off and his heel slipped on the curb.

Drunk and disoriented, he went down hard on his ass. He grunted, but instead of trying to get up, he simply lay on his back and stared up at the darkening sky.

And then he started to laugh.

It was only a chuckle at first, but it soon degenerated into a belly rumbling guffaw. A few seconds after that, he realized that he was crying.

Not sobbing, exactly, but crying hard enough for tears to stream down his cheeks.

A shadowy figure suddenly loomed over him, and he blinked the tears away. With the fading sun behind him, Drake couldn't make out his face, but he saw that the man was holding a hand out to him.

"You okay, mister?"

Drake laughed again and somehow managed to articulate that he was fine.

"Let me help you up, then," the man said in a gentle voice. Drake shrugged and grabbed his hand. The man was thin, but his grip was strong, and when he yanked, Drake was hoisted to his feet.

He then proceeded to dust himself off.

"Thanks," he said, trying his best not to slur.

"No problem," the man responded. "You should be careful out here, especially if you've been drinking. Not everyone is as nice as I am."

Drake squinted, trying to make out the man's face. He saw a narrow nose, deep-set eyes, and the beginnings of a beard. But try as he might, he was just too drunk to get a good overall idea of him.

"I'll be fine," he said, but the man was already gone.

***

Drake somehow made it all the way to his couch without falling again. This took every ounce of his strength, and when he saw the worn leather, he collapsed into it, breathing long and deep.

He lay there for a long while, each successive blink lasting longer than the previous.

Sleep threatened to overtake him, and he was prepared to welcome it. But just as he felt his neck droop, the phone in his pocket buzzed. Normally he wouldn't answer it, but thoughts of Alyssa forced his hand.

And drunk as he was, he wasn't too drunk to see her again.

Only after he managed to remove the phone from his pocket, dropping it twice in the process, he realized that he hadn't even given the woman his number.

It wasn't her; it was another message from Beckett. This time, however, he didn't even bother to read it.

"Leave me alone," he grumbled as he deleted the message.

He was about to lean back again and allow sleep to come, when he spied the icon that looked like a miniature video camera on his home screen. Drake pressed it with his thumb.

A window popped open, but instead of the one bisected screen, he saw five extra icons.

Screech must have set up the cameras in the other homes already, he thought with a hint of pride.

Screech was a good man. Strange, odd-looking, and he had a brutally annoying laugh, but he was a good man.

Drake was lucky to have found him.

He wasn't interested in the other icons, just the first. He clicked it and then stared at the upper right-hand corner of the screen.

Mrs. Armatridge was in bed, her husband lying beside her. They had their backs to each other, and as far as he could tell beneath their thick, quilted bedspread, they didn't appear to be touching.

And yet they had something that Drake wanted very much.

Can I be like that one day? Can I fall in love with someone and live to be old, to be happy?

They weren't touching, but they appeared *peaceful*.

The phone slipped from Drake's hand and his head slumped back against the couch.

He fell asleep.

A sweet, dreamless sleep.

Chapter 28

CHASE SHOWED UP HER badge to the nearest officer.

"Detective Adams," she said, then gestured to the man behind her. "And this is Dr. Campbell."

The officer nodded and stepped aside. Chase and Beckett strode forward, and the uniform fell into step beside them.

"The victim is a male in his early twenties. Appears to have died from a self-inflicted gunshot wound to the cheek; there's a massive exit wound on the top of his skull. His given name is Gerald Leblanc, but he occasionally went by Geraldine."

Chase raised an eyebrow and the police officer, sensing her confusion, continued.

"Street worker. I knew the man, picked him up a few times. Nice kid, confused, sure, but a nice kid. I just never thought…" he let his sentence trail off.

Halfway down the alleyway now, Chase stopped and turned to face the officer.

"You going to be alright Officer…"

"Dwight."

"You going to be alright Officer Dwight?"

The man made a face.

"I'll be fine."

With a nod, they continued forward again at a brisk clip, making their way toward a dumpster that was cordoned off by police tape.

Officer Dwight cleared his throat.

"A couple passersby heard the shot and called it in. Nobody came down the alley—and no one saw anyone exit—until the first officer was on scene."

A sudden series of dull thuds suddenly filled the air, and Chase turned her gaze skyward.

"Was that thunder?"

"No, ma'am," replied Officer Dwight. "There's a bar up the street… supper club type of thing. Barney's, I think. Music pounds from four in the afternoon 'till four in the morning."

Chase checked her watch. It was six pm.

"Well it's annoying as hell," she replied, moving closer to the dumpster.

Beckett grunted his agreement.

She cleared the edge of the dumpster and despite being prepared for what was to come, the scene still took her by surprise.

It wasn't the gore, that much she had become accustomed to. It was the uncanny resemblance to the photograph that had lain on Beckett's desk.

Gerald was on his back, arms laying at his sides. In fact, from the chin down, she might have thought him sleeping. His chest was bare, and his skin was puckered from the cold, and he was wearing a pair of dark jeans.

Even the lower part of his face looked normal, complete with reddish stubble. But when she raised her gaze just a little higher, things went from ordinary to grotesque.

There was a dime-sized hole on his left cheek, rimmed with dried blood. From there, things got progressively worse. The man's eyes were rolled back, revealing mostly whites. The top of his head was completely obliterated: it was a ragged mess of flesh and blood that spread out across the pavement like a bowl of spilled fettuccine. Brain matter clung to the side of the dumpster like oatmeal.

"That the weapon?" Chase asked, kneeling beside an old-fashioned rifle. It was lying with the barrel pointed away from the body next to his right arm.

"Looks like it," Officer Dwight replied.

"I was asking Beckett," Chase said sharply.

Beckett picked up the gun with a gloved hand and inspected the barrel. After several moments, he replaced it in the same position, then went to inspect Gerald's face. He probed the skin around the bullet hole, then used his pinky to determine the size of the entrance wound.

"It's consistent. Won't be able to tell for sure until we get it to the lab." He removed what looked like a wet-nap from his pocket, opened it, then ran it across the index finger and thumb of Gerald's pale hand.

Beckett waited for five seconds, then held the paper up for Chase to see.

It was covered in gray smudges.

"GSR on his hands."

Chase nodded as Beckett stood and started to root through his black medical bag. As he rummaged, she observed the scene in more detail, trying to find something—anything—that would suggest foul play.

Her breath made frosty puffs in the air, and she shivered.

The temperature was dropping.

"Why isn't he wearing a shirt?" she asked.

"Excuse me?"

Chase turned to look at Officer Dwight.

"Why isn't he wearing a shirt? It's getting cold out here."

Dwight shrugged.

"I don't, I guess—"

Chase interrupted him.

"Look in the dumpster."

"Ah, pardon?"

Chase sighed.

"Take a look in the dumpster, see if you can find his shirt."

"Yes ma'am," he said, then immediately moved to the dumpster and threw the top back. It clanged loudly and Chase cringed.

"Hey, Chase?" Beckett said.

"What is it?"

"Check this out," he replied, holding a manila folder open to him. She only needed to glance at the photograph to realize that the similarities were uncanny: the bullet hole in Gerald's left cheek, the obliterated top of his head. The bare chest, the dark jeans.

She closed her eyes and pressed her fingers to her temples.

"Found something!"

Chase opened her eyes and looked over at Officer Dwight. He was using some sort of stick that he had found in the dumpster to hold up a sequined muscle shirt.

"This is his. I picked him up wearing this very shirt a couple of months back."

Chase felt a headache coming on, and she ground her teeth against it.

"Want me to bag it?" Dwight asked. And then, before she could answer, he turned to Beckett, "Can we wrap this up here? Mark it up as a suicide?"

Chase took an aggressive step forward.

"Suicide? *Suicide?* Who takes off their shirt before committing suicide? Does that make sense to you? What, Gerald didn't want to get his clothes dirty before he died?"

Dwight looked scared.

"I'm sorry—"

"Maybe he was worried about the dry-cleaning bill. Shit, they might charge extra for cleaning blood and brain matter from sequins." She leaned into the man, feeling her emotions start to bubble over. "Is that what he was doing, Dwight?"

The officer averted his eyes.

"I just thought—"

"You *thought?* You thought, what? That he—"

Beckett's hand came down on her shoulder, and she paused to look over at him. His lips were pressed together tightly.

Chase shook her head.

"I'm sorry," she said to Officer Dwight. "But this is no suicide. I want CSU in here; I want them to comb the whole goddamn alley. As far as the damn bar that keeps playing that obnoxious music, even. This, Officer Dwight, isn't a suicide; it's a homicide."

Chapter 29

WHEN DRAKE FIRST OPENED his eyes, he wasn't completely sure where he was. He blinked rapidly, trying to break the gumminess that held his lids together, and when that failed, he rubbed them with his fingers.

I'm on the couch, he realized. He tried to rise, but his head started to ache and he sat back down.

"Shit," he grumbled. He clucked his tongue, and his stomach lurched.

Somehow, he made it to the kitchen, where he chased two Advil with a glass of warm water. As he waited for the medicine to take effect, he had a cool shower and got dressed.

"What the hell happened last night?" he asked himself. He remembered going to the bar, to Barney's, but he didn't remember coming home.

He had no idea why his ass was sore, either, which was something of a concern for him. Just thinking of how *that* might have happened made him cringe.

By the time he was finally dressed and ready, it was nearing ten o'clock. He scooped his phone off the table and saw that the red light was once again blinking. It seemed like every time he picked the damn thing up he had messages waiting. Drake was beginning to think that letting Screech convince him that he needed a smartphone, when he was technologically dumb, wasn't the best idea.

So long as it's not Beckett again.

It wasn't.

It was a message from Screech, and Drake read it out loud.

Drake where you at? It's nine-thirty and Mrs. Armatridge has been waiting for nearly an hour and I'm running out of prune juice to offer!

He shook his head, chuckled, and then hurried outside to his rusty Crown Vic.

***

Screech's voice reached him even though the door to Triple D was firmly closed.

"I'm sure Drake will be here any minute, Mrs. Armatridge. He's probably... he's probably doing some police work. You know he used to be a police officer—a detective, don't you?"

Drake put his hand on the doorknob but didn't immediately open the door. Instead, he listened.

"Yes, I know he was a detective. But not anymore. He works for me now. And you've been telling me the same thing for the past hour."

"Can I get you anything while you wait? A *pastille* maybe?"

He heard the elderly woman scoff.

"Pastille? That would do wonders for my IBS. How about a glass of water? Filtered, of course. Perrier would be even better."

Drake took a deep breath and put on his best smile. Then he opened the door.

Mrs. Armatridge was sitting in one of the burgundy chairs, Screech's crane-like body hovering over her. The other chairs were occupied by more geriatrics.

"Mrs. Armatridge," Drake exclaimed loudly. "I'm so sorry I'm late. Had to help out with the NYPD."

The woman pursed her lips.

"No need to shout. I'm not deaf."

The woman sitting beside Mrs. Armatridge looked over at her and said, "Pardon me?"

Her question went ignored.

"Yes, of course. Please, come into my office," Drake said, trying his best to keep the smile on his face.

The woman pulled herself to her feet, and Drake followed her into his office.

He frowned when he saw the still open bottle of Johnny on the desk and the two glasses. Hurrying around the woman, Drake quickly replaced the cap and put the bottle and glasses in the top drawer of his desk.

"I hope you're still capable of functioning, Damien."

"Yes, of course. I'm sorry for the wait. Now, how can I help you?"

Mrs. Armatridge eyed him from across the desk.

"I see that your office is full, and I suspect that you had more than a few visitors yesterday as well."

Drake admitted as much.

"I think you're smart enough to know that that was my doing, Damien."

"Yes, of course. I want to thank you for your support, Mrs. Armatridge."

Another *hmph*.

"And I just wanted to remind you that I was here first, and I expect that my... how can I say this... my *case* takes precedence."

"Of course."

Drake had no problem swallowing his pride. Four ten thousand dollar checks would do that to a man. And yet something told him that this wasn't the only reason for the woman's visit.

"Is there anything else I can do for you today, Mrs. Armatridge?"

The woman's thin fingers went to the pearls around her neck, and Drake realized that she was nervous.

"I've been reviewing the video from your home."

Her eyes shot up.

"And?"

"And, unfortunately, I have nothing to report at this time."

Mrs. Armatridge's face drooped, and Drake immediately raised a hand to calm her.

"But, I assure you, I've been following the movements of your maid… of Miss Ortiz… very carefully. So far, she appears to be doing nothing but keep the place clean, and look after your husband, of course."

The mention of her husband made her expression harden.

Mrs. Armatridge stood and started toward the door.

That's what this visit was about… a fishing expedition. She wants something to be wrong. She wants me to find something, and won't be satisfied until I do.

"Remember, Damien, how important I have been to your business. And think about how quickly it can all be taken away."

"Yes, of course. I will let you know as soon as I notice something out of the ordinary."

Mrs. Armatridge left his office, and when he heard the outer door open and close, Drake took a deep breath.

"Screech! Send the next one in," he shouted, trying to put the fake smile back on his face.

Chapter 30

BECKETT LEANED OVER THE man with the black spectacles and lab coat.

"Anything?" he asked, trying not to get his hopes up.

The lab technician shook his head.

"Nothing. The man had some alcohol in his system, and traces of marijuana. But nothing at levels that would incapacitate him. Gerald was, however, HIV positive."

Beckett swore and took his hands off the back of the man's chair.

So Gerald was relatively sober when he died.

Tests from the gun lab hadn't come back yet, but Beckett would be shocked if the gun at the scene wasn't the same one that had fired the bullet that had exploded the top of his skull. His wallet was still in his pants, and inside Beckett had found eighty dollars—four twenties.

It didn't look like a robbery was the motive. What it looked like, quite frankly, was a man who was down on his luck. A man who was HIV positive, who was turning tricks for cash and who had just lost the will to live.

And who had ended it all with one bullet.

Beckett rubbed his forehead.

Only that wasn't what happened. What happened was that someone had murdered Gerald Leblanc and made it look like a suicide. Just like what happened to Eddie and the man in the bathtub with the slit wrists, the drunk who asphyxiated, and the woman who OD'd and then drowned in Central Park.

He just had to find *something* that could link the cases, anything that might indicate that their wounds weren't self-inflicted.

"What about the girl in the pond?"

The man in the glasses turned back to his computer and typed away.

"High levels of diamorphine—heroin—in her system. If she hadn't drowned, she most likely would have OD'd."

Beckett swore again.

"And the drunk? The one—ah, fuck it. Never mind," he patted the man on the shoulder, and he jumped. "Thanks for your help."

He turned and started toward the door, intent on leaving the lab.

"Dr. Campbell? Can I ask why you are so interested in these suicides? I mean—"

"No, you may not," he said, without turning back.

***

Beckett stood in the morgue, the four bodies laid on metal gurneys before him. He had found the man from the first image—Trevor Gobbets—and the man in the tub—Nick Thanos—and had reviewed the files from the junior ME as well as the bodies themselves. And his results and conclusions were the same as they had been with Gerald and Eddie.

His gaze skipped from one naked body to the next, his eyes barely focusing on their pale white flesh. That is, until his eyes landed on Eddie's light-brown skin. He shook his head and sighed.

"Goddamn it, Eddie. God-fucking-dammit."

Five murders, all within two weeks.

He loved puzzles, but this one seemed wholly unfair. It was as if all of the pieces had been cut square.

"C'mon Beckett, find *something* to help Chase out. To help Eddie out."

Beckett snapped on his gloves and went to the first body, repeating the same process he had done at least a half dozen times already.

Trevor Gobbets had been a homeless man for more than two decades. No family, no friends, no job, no money. The only way they had identified his body was from his fingerprints from a shoplifting charge seven years prior. His corpse showed all the telltale signs of long-term alcoholism: sunken eyes, a pallid complexion, abscesses on his hands and feet. Tox had revealed that he had a blood alcohol level of 0.37. He was so drunk that when he fell on his neck, he didn't wake up.

Or at least that was the way it was made to look.

"How does a homeless alcoholic find enough alcohol to get that drunk?" he wondered out loud. He made a mental note to ask the tech about the specific type of alcohol later. After combing the man's body, and not finding anything in the way of evidence of foul play, he moved on to the next.

Nick Thanos was an obese man who had just recently divorced from his wife and had lost custody of his two children. The narrative was simple: the man was depressed, his life was falling apart, so he decided to off himself by slitting his wrists in the tub.

The cuts on his wrists were deep—deep enough to slice through the tendons. There were three slashes on each wrist, working their way upward, nearly to his elbows. Beckett was about to move on to Eddie next, when he noticed something on the inside of the man's right hand. Sliding down the body to get a better look, he grabbed the mans forearm and carefully lifted it.

There were callouses on the inside of his thumb and the side of his index finger.

He's right-handed, Beckett thought. He inspected the cuts on his right wrist next, then those on his left. Something wasn't right.

The slashes on the right wrist were strong, deliberate, while those on the left weren't quite as deep, and there appeared to be hesitation marks.

Beckett wasn't positive, but if he were a betting man, he would put his money on the fact that Nick had cut his *right* wrist first. Which, being right-handed, would be very unnatural. It's not much, he figured, but it was *something*.

His phone buzzed in his pocket and he lowered the corpse's arm back to the gurney, pulled off his glove, and answered it.

"Yeah?" he said, surprised at how tired he sounded.

"Dr. Campbell? It's Zeke."

Zeke? Who the hell is Zeke?

"Who?"

"Zeke? From the lab? We just spoke ten minutes ago."

"Ah, sure, Zeke. What is it?"

"So I was taking another look at Trevor Gobbets's tox?"

He had Beckett's full attention now.

"And? What did you find?"

"Well, I'm not sure if it's anything, but I was looking at the numbers again, and it looks like he had trace amounts of methanol in his system."

"Methanol? You sure?"

"Yep. I'm sure, I mean it could—"

"Thanks, Zeke, big help," Beckett said and then hung up the phone.

Then he immediately dialed Chase's number.

It appeared as if the puzzle pieces had finally acquired a familiar shape.

Chapter 31

"**Wait, slow down, Beckett.** Methanol? What does that mean?" Chase asked in a hushed tone. As she waited for Beckett to reply, she rose and went to her office door and closed it. Then she opened two sets of photographs—one from the crime scenes, and one from the forensic pathology exam.

Beckett continued after a deep breath.

"Most people don't know this, but the ethanol used in labs is spiked with five percent methanol to prevent people from drinking the damn stuff. And our first vic, Trevor Gobbets, had some in his system. The way I figure it, whoever killed him wanted to get him super drunk, super fast and added ethanol to his drink."

Chase mulled this over.

"He was poisoned then?"

"Looks that way. There's no way of proving that Trevor didn't just come across the ethanol on his own, but it's a start. And there's one more thing. The man in the bathtub? He's right-handed, and yet I'm pretty sure his right wrist was slashed first."

"I'm not sure I follow."

"Try it. Grab a pencil or something."

Chase picked up a pencil in her right hand and instinctively brought it to her left wrist. And then she understood.

"Yeah, it would be natural for a right-handed person to cut his left wrist first."

"Exactly."

Chase stared at the pictures as she spoke, trying to imagine Nick's last thought before he cut his wrists. A shudder ran through her.

"It's no smoking gun," she said at last. "But you're right. It is something."

"Enough to take to Rhodes?" Beckett asked.

Chase sighed. It wasn't enough, not even close. She suspected that they could have a confession from a convicted murderer and that still might not be enough.

"Yes," she lied. "Enough to take it to him, anyway. Whether he goes for it, that's another story."

There was a long pause, during which time Chase scooped up the pictures and put them back in their respective folders.

"Beckett, you still there?"

"Yep."

"I'm going to take it to Rhodes. I'll let you know how it goes," she said as she made her way toward the door.

"Oh, one more thing? Remember when I asked you about the photographer at the Central Park vic?"

Chase thought back to that night, of the scuba diver who broke the surface of the water and gave her the ironic thumb's up sign.

"Yeah, what about him?"

"Did you ever manage to get the pics?"

"No, I couldn't find him, actually. We have the pics that the officer took when you were there, but not the ones from before you arrived."

There was a moment of silence.

"I think I'm more interested in the photographer now than the pictures," he said at last. "Anyways, see if you can find him. And good luck with Rhodes. Call me afterward."

Chase hung up the phone and took a deep breath. Then she stepped into the hallway and made her way toward Sergeant Rhodes's office.

***

"No—no way in hell, Chase. Besides, three of these deaths have already been ruled suicides or accidents."

"So? So, what? There are no statutes on murder and this wouldn't be the first time that a suicide was deemed a murder after the fact."

Sergeant Rhodes leaned forward and planted his elbows on his desk. He interlaced his long, thin fingers, a gesture that served no other purpose but to unnerve and annoy Chase.

It worked; she could feel the blood starting to flood into her cheeks.

"Please, Detective Adams, feel free to lecture me further on the minutia of the law. Go on, don't be shy."

Chase clenched her teeth together, trapping a snide remark behind them. Rhodes blinked slowly, his eyes bulging slightly from behind his round spectacles.

"Ah, good. Now, you want to know what I think?"

Chase figured that the question was rhetorical, and didn't answer.

"I think," Rhodes continued after a prolonged delay, "that you're getting a bit antsy. I think that after Dr. Kruk, you got an inkling for serial killers, hmm? Maybe you think that media attention is the only way to the top?"

Chase swallowed hard.

Inkling for serial killers? Is he fucking serious?

"Mm, hmm. Things are too calm for you? Too quiet? Not interested in gangbangers shooting themselves for crack money?"

Chase squinted hard. She felt a pressure building deep in the pit of her stomach. She was about to explode—if Rhodes continued on this line of patronizing bullshit, the consequences of her actions might soon become an afterthought.

Thankfully, the diatribe changed directions.

"Look, Chase. I like you, and I think you are an excellent detective, which is why I promoted you to first grade faster than anyone in the history of this department. I'm going to let you in a little secret. I won't be Sergeant much longer. And this is going to leave an opening, an opening I think that you would be more than qualified to fill."

Rhodes paused and stared at her. Chase wasn't sure how to respond, so she elected to say nothing.

After a few moments, he continued.

"As a Sergeant, and with a recommendation from the newly instated Lieutenant, and maybe even the mayor, I'm sure it would be no problem to transfer to Quantico, if you catch my drift."

Chase exhaled.

Rhodes knew about her aspirations for the FBI, her growing interest in criminal profiling. She wasn't sure how, but the bastard *knew*. And now he was blackmailing her with this information.

"Do you understand now, Chase?" he asked, the corners of his mouth turning up into a smile.

Unfortunately, Chase did.

"Yes," she said quietly. "I understand."

She nodded and stood. When she reached across the desk to grab the folder of photographs, Rhodes pulled it out of her reach.

"I think I'll keep these, if that's all right with you."

Chase hesitated.

But then she nodded and left the room.

Oh, she understood alright. She understood that the only thing Rhodes gave a shit about was his own career.

Fortunately for her, Chase also cared about the lives of the New York City citizens.

Chapter 32

BECKETT HAD JUST SAT down at his desk at NYU medical when a frustrated looking Chase burst through the door.

"That bad, huh?"

"What a fucking asshole," she muttered, shaking her head.

"Yeah, that bad."

"Drake was right about him," Chase said, although it wasn't clear if she was simply verbalizing her internal dialog, or if she was expressing her feelings to Beckett.

"Don't blame him, though," he offered.

Chase's eyes darted up.

"What? What do you mean?"

Beckett laid out the photographs again.

"I mean, shit, I know there's a killer out there. But what do we have other than these coincidental images and a few discrepancies? In fact, there are fewer loose ends with these suicides than with many of the other suicides I've cleared over the years."

Chase looked incredulous.

"Tell me you aren't backing out of this now?"

Beckett shook his head.

"Hell no. But with what we have, I'm not surprised that we aren't going to get support from the department, Rhodes or no Rhodes."

Chase looked around the office.

"Where's Suzan?" she asked.

"In class. She's going to do some more digging afterward, though. More digging into Dr. Mrs. Kevorkian."

"Who?"

"Tracey, the woman who took the initial photographs."

Chase nodded.

"Is there anything else, Beckett? Please tell me you have something else."

Beckett sighed.

"I've got nothing."

To his surprise, Chase took this in stride. In fact, it seemed to sober her and her eyes became focused.

"So, what *do* we have, then?" She moved around behind Beckett and pointed at the first photograph. "A dead drunk," she moved to the next image in the sequence, "a depressed obese man, a hanged doctor, a male prostitute who was shot in the face. And then we have a junkie who drowned in Central Park. So…"

"Yeah," Beckett said quietly. "We've got a little game of which one of these aren't like the others."

Chase nodded.

"Your doctor student. The others are drifters, people that wouldn't be missed by society. But Edison… why him? Why kill a young doctor?" Chase asked.

Beckett felt his throat tighten as he heard those words.

Why kill a young doctor?

He still hadn't gotten over the fact that he felt partially responsible for Eddie's death, suicide or not.

If it hadn't been for—

"He's the key, Beckett."

Beckett reluctantly agreed.

"But why kill anyone at all?" he asked. Realizing that his comment was bordering on philosophical, he quickly followed this up with, "I mean, who's the killer? What are his motives?"

Chase chewed her lip.

"A disgruntled student, perhaps? Someone who is trying to get away with the perfect murders?"

Beckett shrugged.

"Maybe—could be. I dunno. But I can tell you one thing, whoever the killer is, he's not going to stop until he completes all eight. And even then, I doubt once he has a taste, he's not going to even stop there."

The image of the babies, illustrated by dolls in Dr. Tracey Moorfield's test prep notes, passed through his mind.

"We have to catch him before he kills again. Only thing is, we can't do this by ourselves. We're going to need help. We're going to need someone who has experience with serial killers, but someone not involved with the NYPD. Someone who doesn't mind bending the rules a little. Know anyone who fits that description?"

Beckett smirked. Even though Chase had asked the question, it was clear that she already knew the answer.

They both did; there was only one man they knew who fit that mold.

"Suzan can't know," Chase said quietly.

"No, she definitely can't find out," Beckett replied.

Part III – Suicide

Chapter 33

"I ASSURE YOU, MRS. Trout, that everything here at Triple D Investigations is done with the utmost discretion. Only myself, my associate, and whomever else you approve will ever see *any* video recordings from inside your home."

Mrs. Trout, a large woman with beady eyes and a nose that continually dripped, smiled, revealing teeth so large that Drake would have bet all of his newly acquired wealth that they were constructed of anything but organic material.

"I have heard great things about you and your company, Damien," Mrs. Trout said in a watery voice before sniffing and then wiping her nose with the sleeve of her white sweater. "And it makes me sleep well at night knowing that you are watching over me."

Drake's eye twitched and he debated telling the woman that he wasn't a private security company and that he was only using the cameras to look for theft, indecent acts and the like. But when the woman grunted and attempted to rise, he bit his tongue and hurried over to her.

Sliding the woman's walker into her thick-knuckled fingers, he said, "Of course. But as with all things in this world, there are no guarantees—other than hard work and discipline, of course."

He smiled as he said this, and Mrs. Trout returned the expression, once again revealing her dentures which were clearly fashioned after Mr. Ed. Up close, her breath reeked of Alka Seltzer and sour cream.

"Thank you, Damien," she said as he held the door open for her.

He stopped smiling the moment she was gone and then collapsed into his chair, motor-boating his lips.

It had been a long morning; after Mrs. Armatridge, he had seen four more of her blue-haired acquaintances, and had spent an ungodly amount of time assuring them of... well, anything that required assurances. And this approach had taken him to unusual places, places that he would have never even fathomed exploring as a detective.

But it also meant four more meaty checks. He had made more money in the past three days than he had in two years as a Detective in the NYPD.

Was it Screech or Alyssa who had asked him if he missed? *Both, I think.*

The answer was becoming more obfuscated with each passing day. The only response that he could offer if put to the question again was wholly unsatisfying, but irrefutably honest: maybe...

His eyes flicked to the growing stacks of checks on his desk.

Or maybe not.

Drake's stomach growled, reminding him that it was past noon and he had yet to eat today.

"Screech?" he hollered. "How 'bout some lunch? I'm buying!"

There was a pause.

"Screech?"

The door to his office suddenly opened, and the man's curly head poked in.

"We have one more client, boss," he said in a strange tone.

"Who? Another one of Mrs. Armatridge's associates?"

Screech shook his head.

"Naw—a man and woman, say they know you. Wouldn't give their names."

Drake's eyes narrowed.

They know me?

"Fine, send them in. In the meantime, go grab some lunch, would you? And then you better stock up on those button recorders. You've got some installation to do today."

Screech laughed and then leaned out the door, motioning for two figures to enter.

Drake smiled too—Screech's laugh, as bizarre as it was, had a way of just making you grin—but when his two newest clients came into view, he immediately frowned.

"Hey Drake," Beckett said with a smirk of his own, "fancy meeting you here. You change your number or something? Because *goddamn* you never seem to answer the damn thing."

Chapter 34

DRAKE WASN'T REALLY SURE how to react.

Should I stand? Shake hands? Hug?

It was strange, given how well he knew Beckett, how *long* he had known him, and how close he and Chase had become even in their short time together. And yet, time apart—six months, short on any global scale—could squeeze more than temporal distance between relationships.

Thankfully, the decision was taken out of his hands.

"Well? Stand the fuck up, you rude bastard and give me a hug," Beckett exclaimed with a smile.

If Drake had any reservations, Beckett striding over to him instantly quashed them. Drake stood then embraced his good friend, clapping him twice on the back. Chase, while less enthusiastic than Beckett, also strode forward, and Drake hugged her as well.

No back claps this time, however.

"Nice digs, Drake," Beckett said, looking around.

Drake chuckled. Triple D Investigations was hardly what he would call 'nice digs'—they were a two-room outfit with peeling paint on the walls in a strip mall that paled in comparison to Dr. Mark Kruk's lavish office—but something told him that maybe, just maybe, Triple D was due for an upgrade. Provided, of course, that the steady stream of paranoid octogenarian women didn't suddenly dry up— literally or figuratively.

Still, Beckett wasn't being mean-spirited; Beckett was just being Beckett.

"Pays the bills—not all of us can pretend to be doctors on TV, you know."

Beckett snorted.

"Touché, my friend."

Chase smiled at him.

"Nice to see you again, Drake. It's been… well, it's been a while."

"It has," Drake replied. "Take a seat guys, for once it'll be me behind the desk. I'll try for best Sergeant Rhodes impression, just to make you comfortable."

Drake had meant his words as a joke, but seeing the way that Chase's face dropped at the mention of Rhodes's name, he knew better than to push it.

He also knew that his two friends weren't here to put up cameras to catch cheating or stealing spouses. For one, Beckett wasn't married and Chase… was she married? Drake wondered. He thought not, but couldn't recall ever asking her directly. She didn't wear a wedding band, that much he knew, but they seemed to be less popular these days, especially for a career woman such as herself.

"Sorry," he said. "Please, sit."

Chase took the seat that Mrs. Trout had vacated moments before, and Beckett pulled one from the side of the room and placed it next to hers.

"Something tells me that this isn't a social call, much as we need to catch up," he offered, trying again to keep the mood light.

"No, it's not," Chase said flatly. "I wish it was, Drake, and I'll be the first to say that I feel terrible about—"

Drake held up a hand silencing her.

"No need, Chase. I didn't call, you didn't call, and Beckett… well, fuck Beckett."

Beckett grunted.

"Oh, I called… and texted and left messages, but someone seems to have a hard time figuring out how to use their phone." Beckett's eyes drifted to Drake's new cell phone that lay on the desk. "But I forgive you. After all, it must be hard operating that thing with your dinosaur claws and lizard brain."

"I'm thirty-eight, Beckett. Less we forget who—"

Beckett made a clucking sound with his tongue.

"A woman never tells."

Drake shook his head in amusement. He was about to add something, but he caught sight of Chase's expression in the corner of his eye and stopped himself. Even though he and Beckett were having a good time ribbing each other, the joviality didn't seem to extend to her.

Chase leaned forward as she spoke.

"But after what happened… you saved my life, Drake. Not only that but you fell on the sword for me, too. And that's something I'll never forget."

Drake nodded briskly, accepting the compliment in stride.

"Alright Prince Fucking Charming," Beckett interrupted, "as the French say, 'let's get to *le* point'." He pulled a folder from his messenger bag and laid it on the table in front of them. When he moved to open it, Drake placed a palm on top.

He sighed heavily before speaking.

"Guys, I know that I'm going to come off sounding like a dick, but, please—*please*—don't open the file." Chase started to protest, but Drake continued, "Like I said, I'm a dick, I get it. But I've been through a lot, and I'm happy to say that I've moved on. Moved on from a lot of things, actually."

An awkward silence fell over the quaint office. It suddenly felt too tight for Drake, too constricted, and he was beginning to think that a move might happen sooner rather than later.

Slowly, with one eyebrow raised, Beckett peeled Drake's hand from the top of the manila folder.

"Okay, Eeyore, keep your panties on. We just want to show you a few images. Get your opinion on a couple of things. That's all. We're not entrusting you with North Korea's nuke codes, alright?"

Beckett's act was flawless, and Drake would have fallen for it, too, if it hadn't been for Chase. The woman's green eyes darted over at Beckett as he spoke, giving them both away.

And I thought you were the poker player, Chase? He thought absently.

Regardless, while Drake might be a dick, he wasn't a prick. He leaned back in his chair and held his hands up, admitting surrender.

"First consultation's free," he said. But when Beckett flipped the folder open, Drake realized that this was no joking matter.

Chase leaned forward and spread five photographs on his desk.

"Two weeks, five dead bodies," she said simply and then paused.

Drake, realizing that she wanted his immediate input, leaned forward and briefly glanced at each one of the photographs in sequence. When he was done, he said, "A bunch of people committed suicide. That's what you came here for?"

"Ha!" Beckett exclaimed, turning to Chase. "See? Told ya. You owe me twenty."

Chase frowned and shook her head.

"What? What am I missing?" Drake asked.

"Nothing," Chase replied, shooting a look at Beckett. She took out another folder and laid another series of photographs above the ones that Beckett had displayed.

Drake looked them over, his brow furrowing in confusion.

"I don't get it—they're the same."

"Ah, my dear Watson, they are *not* the same. Close, but that only counts in horseshoes and hand-grenades my friend. And this is neither. This is murder."

Chapter 35

NUMBER SIX WAS PROBABLY the most difficult to recreate. The man knew this; he knew it even before starting this entire task by slipping the ethanol into Trevor's drink. But he was up for the challenge. After all, he had had more than a decade to plan this out. Fifteen years to study, to research, to plan.

Electrocution required very specific equipment and very important safety measures. After all, he couldn't die slitting someone else's wrists, hanging someone, or shooting them in the face. But electrocution? One little mistake, one simple touch that lasted a second too long, and the current would enter his body as well. Only for a split-second, mind you, but that was all the time needed to fry his organic circuit board.

Yes, electrocution required a special sort of technique.

But he was up for the challenge.

The man wound down his window several inches as the tow truck driver approached.

"I don't know what happened, mister," he said with a shrug. "It just… it just *stopped*. It was in the shop a few weeks ago, and they said something about the cables going to the battery—corroded? Does that sound right? Anyway, I didn't do anything about it, because I just thought that they were trying to stick me for more cash, you know?"

The left side of the tow truck driver's upper lip curled.

"Should always listen to your mechanic," he replied in a gruff voice.

The man in the car put a hand to his chest.

"I know, I know. A lesson lived is a lesson learned, as they say."

The driver muttered something under his breath, something that sounded to the man in the car like, *fucking queer*, and then went to the front of the car.

"Pop the hood," he shouted, scratching at an oil stain on his over-sized t-shirt.

"No problem," the man hollered out the window as he pulled the hood release. "You know what? Let me help you."

The tow truck driver held up a meaty palm before raising the hood.

"Nah, that's alright, stay in the car."

"No, no," the man in the driver seat said, a smile on his face. "I insist."

Chapter 36

Drake suddenly understood Chase's expression when he had made the joke about Sergeant Rhodes.

"Lemme guess," he said, "Rhodes didn't want to touch this with a ten-foot pole."

Beckett scoffed.

"Rhodes wouldn't touch this with a goddamn Kraken tentacle."

Drake shook his head and made a face.

What the hell does that even mean?

Rather than humoring Beckett, however, he turned his attention back to the images on his desk. He was still having a hard time seeing how they were different; to him, it looked like the same crime scenes, only the photographs were taken at slightly different angles. Which would make sense; he'd been at hundreds of crime scenes, and the photographers weren't shy with their trigger fingers.

"Anyways, you sure that these aren't, uh, natural—I mean, as much as suicide and accidents can be considered natural?"

"There's no way," Chase replied. "It's not just the similarity, but it's the order in which they occurred. First the, uh—"

"Asphyxia," Beckett offered.

"—asphyxia, all the way to the gunshot wound. Next is electrocution. Problem is, Drake, we've got nothing. And with Rhodes being… what's the word… *resistant*, we aren't going to get anything. That's why we need your help."

Drake looked at Chase, at the photographs, then at Beckett. They were desperate, he saw, and despite his reservations, he could feel something tug at him the way a fat kid might pull a polo shirt that hugged him just a little too tightly around the hips.

Short, nagging little tweaks.

They needed him, and he felt the urge to help.

"This here looks like a drunk," he said, pointing at the first photograph then to the drowning victim, "and this one's definitely a junkie. What about the others, they all the same?"

Beckett shook his head.

"That's what Chase and I discussed earlier. They're all the same, except," he planted a finger on the man hanging from the ceiling, his back to the photographer, "this one."

"And?" Drake asked, "What's so different about this guy?"

Something changed in Beckett's face. It seemed to pinch somehow, fold in on itself.

"This guy's a doctor. A student of mine."

And with that, everything came flooding back: Dr. Edison Larringer's visit, spouting off about suicides that weren't really suicides, and Drake telling him to take a hike, to go to the police if he thought crimes had been committed.

"No," he moaned, unable to control himself.

"Drake? You alright?" Chase asked, but her voice seemed far away. Very, very far away. Tunnel vision closed in just as Beckett jumped to his feet. He clapped a hand against Drake's back as if he were choking.

"Drake? What the hell's wrong with you? *Drake!*"

Drake shook his head and snapped back to reality.

"Please tell me this isn't," he racked his brain for the name, "Eddie."

Now it was Beckett's turn to be shocked.

"What? You knew him?"

Drake didn't answer right away. Instead, he resolved himself to just shaking his head over and over again, until he got dizzy and his hangover returned with renewed fervor.

"Yeah, I know him. At least, I met him. He came in here about a week ago."

Chase shot to her feet.

"*What?* What did he say? Why was he here?"

Drake licked his lips, which suddenly felt dry nearly to the point of cracking.

"Dr. Edison… Larringer? I think his name was Larringer—he came here with the exact same story that you guys are telling me now: a photograph of a suicide he thinks was actually a murder. Said he was a student of yours."

Beckett gawked.

"What? For real? Why didn't you tell me?"

Drake shook his head.

"I told the—shit, I told the young doctor to go to the police, that I wasn't a cop anymore."

"And what'd he say?" Chase asked.

"Said he couldn't go to the police, that if he did he would get his medical license revoked—that's what I think he said, anyway."

"Why?"

"Because he stole the images from you, Beckett. He was trying to cheat on the test, and he took them from your desk."

All of the air was sucked from Beckett's lungs, leaving him with an expression that reminiscent of what Drake thought Mrs. Trout might look like sans dentures.

Drake himself was not exempt from the horrible realization that Eddie was dead, that he might have been the last one to see the young doctor alive. His heart started to race in his chest as he thought back to a day that which, while it couldn't have been more than a week ago, felt like it had happened a decade or more prior.

And I know one thing for certain: that man… he didn't die from positional asphyxia. He was murdered.

Drake had turned Eddie away. Like a pauper scorning an unworthy peasant, he had sent him away.

Now he was dead.

Murdered.

Memories of Clay came flooding back then, a deluge that threatened to drown him.

Should we announce our presence? Say that we are NYPD?

It's your case, Clay, you decide. This is a waste of time, anyway.

"Tell me everything he said," Beckett whispered. "I want to know everything."

Chapter 37

AN UNCOMFORTABLE SILENCE SETTLED over the room after Drake had recounted his interactions with Dr. Edison Larringer. Part of him felt the need to defend himself, to say, *'hell, it isn't my problem, none of this was my fault. I'm no longer a detective with the NYPD'*, but he knew that this was simply a defense mechanism that would only lead to self-pity or, worse, self-loathing.

And lord knows, he had enough of both to last a lifetime.

"I'll help you," he said at last. "Whatever you need, I'll help you catch the killer."

Beckett nodded solemnly. It was clear to Drake that like him, Beckett also harbored guilty feelings about the young doctor's death.

"We have to stop him before he strikes again," Chase said quietly.

"Do we have any suspects?"

She shook her head.

"None. But the images from the test? They were restricted. Only students could see them."

"What do you mean, *could* see them?" Drake asked.

It was Beckett who answered.

"I asked the professor who posted them to take them down, which narrows our suspect pool to either a current or past student. That being said, I tried to gain access to student records, tried to get a friend in the IT department to give me a list, but he said no dice. Tighter than a nun's —" his eyes darted to Chase, "—than a nun's, uh, church bible. Anyway, I know who took the class this year and last, and can probably dig up names from a few semesters before that, but that's about it."

Chase nodded.

"I asked Officer Dunbar to do a little digging. He's going to try and cross-reference the names that Beckett provided with criminal records, but he can only look superficially. He's paranoid that Rhodes is watching him, and with good reason after what happened with the Butterfly Killer."

"Huh," Drake grumbled. "So it's all on me, is it?"

A thought occurred to him then.

"Beckett, reach back and open my office door, would you?"

Beckett nodded and opened it.

"Screech, can you come in here for a sec?"

In an instant, Screech appeared in the doorway.

"What is it, boss?" he asked, and Drake felt his face redden.

Boss; that's what I used to call Chase as a joke.

"Just get in here. I need you to meet some people."

Screech entered, and after introductions, Drake got his partner up to speed.

"So we're looking for an ex-student, huh?" Screech asked.

Drake was surprised by the immediacy of his response. He looked to Chase first, then Beckett. After a nod from the former, he said, "Considering the restricted nature of the slides, yeah I think that's the best place to start."

"Not only that," Beckett added, "but whoever's doing this, whoever's recreating these suicides, has considerable medical and scientific knowledge. He knows exactly how to kill these people to make them look like suicides, down to the angle of the ligature, to the amount of time to submerge the body in water. And so far CSU hasn't found a hair, a fiber, any DNA at all consistent across crime scenes. I mean, I signed off on some of these as suicides before I knew about all of this, for Christ's sake."

Screech put his hands together and cracked his knuckles.

"Well, I can't say that national espionage is my specialty, but I'm game."

Drake didn't share his partner's enthusiasm, despite what had happened to Dr. Edison Larringer.

Chase apparently picked up on his apprehension, as she said, "Drake, I know what happened. I know what happened with Clay, with the Skeleton King, and what happened with Dr. Kruk. I can't imagine the toll that has taken on you. But we need your help. I wouldn't ask if…" she let her sentence trail off.

Drake bit his tongue. Chase knew what happened with the Butterfly Killer, of course, but she had no clue about the Skeleton King.

No one did.

Except for him and Clay, and Clay was dead.

And his killer was still out there; no matter what anyone said, Peter Kellington was not the Skeleton King.

Drake knew that if he helped Chase and Beckett, that his nightmares would return, and that chasing their killer wouldn't be enough.

He would be compelled to find the man responsible for Clay's death, as well.

If it didn't kill him first.

Chapter 38

"I THINK I SEE the problem," the tow truck driver said as he leaned under the hood. "It looks like… it looks like your battery has been disconnected from the alternator."

"Really? How is that possible?"

The tow truck driver, who after considerable prying the man had discovered was named Toby, shrugged.

"You been into the shop lately?"

The man admitted he had.

"They said that my battery was running low, that I might have to replace it soon."

Toby chuckled.

"Scammers. Without the alternator connected, your battery will die in an hour or so. Quicker if you have the heat on or play the radio."

"Huh. Well, ain't that a pickle. Can you help me?"

"I can boost you, but it'll only last long enough to get you to the shop. Like I said, an hour, tops."

"What about reconnecting the alternator? Can you do that?"

Toby leaned further into the engine.

"Looks like the bastards took all the cables. I'll see if I can find something in my truck."

With that, Toby spun away from the open hood and went back to his truck to rummage in the cab. As he did, the man grabbed the yellow bag containing a brand new set of jumper cables off the front seat of his car. Then he quickly left his vehicle and went back to his post by the open hood, cables in hand.

Toby returned, a sour expression pulling his jowls down low.

"Sorry but I don't have the right wires to reconnect it. But like I said, I can boost you so that you can start the engine... and I see you have cables. Great."

The man nodded.

"Ph, alright then. Should I connect them...?"

Toby's scowl became a patronizing smirk.

"Yeah, don't worry about it. I'll take care of it." Toby strode forward as he spoke and took the cables from his outstretched hand and teased them out of the bag.

"Thank you. This is... well, embarrassing, I guess."

Toby chuckled.

"Don't worry about it—it's not your fault. Some asshole mechanic just took advantage of you. Happens all the time."

He proceeded to connect the red and black leads to the man's car battery.

"Alright," he said, breathing on his hands to warm them. "I'm going to connect them to my battery now. You sit in the car, and when I give you the signal, start it up, okay?"

"Yeah, sure. Thank you," the man said with a smile. Toby nodded and then went back to his car, while the man did the same.

When he was alone in the driver's seat, the man put the keys in the ignition and turned them halfway. The lights on the dash lit up.

That's step one... Toby didn't even check to see if the battery was still live.

And of course, the battery was fine.

The man took a deep breath, then peered out the windshield. He waited until Toby gave him the thumbs up sign, before poking his tongue into his cheek. He pretended to turn the key a few times and, content that Toby had bought his little charade, he started the car.

The engine roared to life.

The man threw his hands up—*success!*—and then got out of his car. Moving quickly, he went to his engine even before Toby managed to haul himself out of his oversized truck. But instead of removing both jumper cables, he only teased the red one off.

And this is step two, the man thought, his breathing becoming more rapid.

With a trembling hand, he moved the clamp toward the alternator. After several deep breaths, he grit his teeth and snapped the lead onto the rectifier. There was a brief shower of sparks, but he managed to pull his hand back before he got burned. The headlights of his car dimmed slightly, and an electrical fizz filled the air beneath the hood, but the man paid this little heed. Behind him, he heard the sound of Toby opening his door, and he spun around.

"I got it! I got it!" the man said with a large smile, waving his hand to reinforce his words.

When Toby frowned and continued to lower his large body from his truck, the man broke into a near sprint.

Step three...

He made it to the tow truck before Toby had cleared the front of the car. With another, hitching breath, he reached for the leads still attached to the battery. A caustic foam started to ooze from the positive terminal, working itself into an angry froth.

The man hesitated.

"You should probably leave that to the professionals," Toby said, suddenly behind him.

"Oh, that's alright. I've got to learn sometime, you know? And you've been such a good help," the man replied as he grabbed the rubber handles of both jumper cable clips. He half expected to feel a jolt, a thrum of electricity course through his fingers and up his arms, but when this didn't happen, his heart rate seemed to slow a little.

"Did you... hey, did you remove the cables from your car?" Toby asked. "And what's that smell?"

"Yes, of course, I thought—"

The man spun around as he spoke, leading with the charged jumper cables.

Toby, seeing the expression on the man's face, tried to pull back, but he was too fat, too slow. The red clip pinched on his neck, the black on his shoulder.

Toby's eyes went wide and he immediately swatted at the leads, but his arms seemed to freeze in mid-air, his elbows seized at awkward angles.

Something between a croak and a gasp escaped Toby's now pale lips, and then it was as if his body had been liquefied. He collapsed to the gravel road in a heap. A second later, his back arched so far that only the man's shoulder blades and hips remained in contact with the ground as electricity coursed through him.

Satisfied that the clips wouldn't slip, the man quickly made his way to his car and leaped into the driver's seat.

Teeth gritted, he jammed his foot against the gas pedal, causing the engine to rev and the dome light above him to blink out.

Toby's back arched even greater, and smoke began to rise from his cavernous mouth. When the man eased his foot off the gas, the tow truck driver's body collapsed to the ground again. He gunned the engine a second time, and this time didn't ease up until he could smell burning flesh in the air.

Electrocution was the most difficult scene to replicate, but it had gone off without a hitch.

The man smiled, then stepped back onto the gravel road. After observing his work for several seconds, he set about manufacturing the scene.

Chapter 39

"You're paying me extra for this," Screech said. "Mad extra. In fact, I want double."

Drake chuckled.

"What? You think that this is without risks?" Screech asked, his eyes wide.

Beckett had since gone back to the morgue, and Chase to 62nd precinct, leaving Drake and Screech alone in the office to discuss what they were going to do next. Screech had been gung-ho about getting involved when Beckett and Chase were present, but now that they had gone he seemed to be getting cold feet.

Drake himself was still having a hard time coming to grips with the fact that the young doctor that had been in his office not more than a week ago had been murdered.

Detective or not, Drake was still a good man and he felt the familiar pressure of responsibility for what had happened to Eddie.

And this was going to drive him to find the killer.

I need a fucking drink, he thought with a grimace.

"Double?" he said, all of a sudden feeling tired.

Screech folded his arms over his narrow chest, his lips pressing together tightly.

"Shit, yeah." His eyes darted to the checks that still lay on Drake's desk. After all that had happened, Mrs. Armatridge and her cronies's problems seemed inconsequential. And every moment that the killer remained on the loose, they grew even more insignificant.

The money, however, was what kept Triple D's doors open.

"Double," Screech repeated. He was trying to look obstinate, like a man negotiating the sale of a used car. Except he only looked like a little boy, one who was mad because Mommy wouldn't give him a second scoop of ice cream.

The expression almost made Drake laugh, and he would have if copies of five photographs of the victims weren't laid out on his desk like tarot cards.

"How about half?" he countered.

Screech made a face.

"Half?"

Drake nodded and shrugged at the same time.

"Half."

"What the hell are you talking about, half? Half of what?"

Drake paused.

"Half of Triple D."

Screech was trying his best to remain calm, but Drake could literally see his body rock as his heart pounded away in his chest.

"One... one and a half D's?" Screech asked with a hint of a smile.

"Half the company, you dork."

Screech tilted his head and closed one eye.

"Three-quarters," he said, then followed this quickly with, "Just fucking with you."

Screech held out his hand and Drake grabbed it and shook hard.

"We have a deal, Drake," Screech said. "Now can we just change the name to something slightly less erotic? DDS Investigations, maybe?"

"What are we? A couple of dentists? The name stays, Screech."

"Alright, alright."

"Good, now go set up more cameras for the prune juicers, will you? Then, after you've done that, see what you can dig up on old forensic pathology students."

Screech nodded and stood. He was partway to the door when he turned and said, "What about you?"

"I'm going to find a killer," Drake replied, all the humor gone from his voice.

"Oh, sure, you take the easy job."

Chapter 40

BECKETT LEFT DRAKE AND Triple D with an uneasy feeling in the pit of his stomach. He and Chase had gone there with the intention of recruiting Drake, and while this took some cajoling, not only had they succeed, but they had also obtained the services of his partner, the weird, curly-headed man with the annoying laugh, and yet it still didn't feel right.

The fact that Eddie had been there, that he had visited Drake before he was murdered, struck a chord with him.

Beckett had stayed with Drake even after what had happened to Clay, despite the fact that Clay was his friend as well, because he *knew* Drake. He knew Drake was a good man. Sure, he bent the rules every now and again, skirted the knife edge of morality and law, but that was because his pursuits were noble.

But with Eddie… if Drake had only listened to him, then he would probably still be alive today. Hell, all he had to do was give Beckett a call. Was that too much to ask?

Within the hour, Beckett found himself back at the morgue, standing alone in the room with the five bodies that he was now convinced had been murdered. It was cool in the morgue, and although Eddie's body had yet to decompose as it would if it had been exposed to the elements, his eyes still bulged unnaturally and his skin had acquired the pallor of milk spilled on a marble countertop.

Beckett knew that he was missing something, that there was something here, some clue on the bodies, but he had stared at them for so long now that he was blind to them.

It was time for another set of eyes. Young eyes; young inexperienced eyes.

His first thought was the fellow that he had left in charge when he had gone to Montreal a few months back—*what the hell was his name? Reggie? Archibald? Greg?*—but he immediately scratched that off the list. After all, the fellow would have known Eddie, known him well.

No, it had to be someone else.

It had to be Suzan.

As much as it pained him to get her involved again, especially considering that Drake was now on board, it just *had* to be her. Sure, there were many others that were more qualified, including Dr. Tracey Moorfield, but he also needed to exercise discretion. He had yet to release the bodies, and although he hadn't been explicitly told to get things moving in this regard, he could feel the pressure coming down the chain of command.

Senior Medical Examiner of NYC still had to report to the Chief Medical Examiner, and that relationship was one that he valued very much.

Beckett took off a glove and pulled out his phone.

He scrolled quickly through the contacts until he found Suzan's number.

"Suzan? It's Beckett. Think you can come down to the morgue? There's something I need your opinion on…"

***

"These are the bodies?" Suzan asked quietly.

Beckett nodded. He had pulled the sheets over the corpses before she had arrived, and now he stood back, allowing Suzan to take her time while she observed their outlines on the metal gurneys.

"Those are them," he replied. "All five, in the same order as the test—in the order that they died."

Suzan nodded and walked over to the first gurney, running her finger along the silver edge, tilting her head pensively.

It occurred to him then that these were probably the first, or one of the first, dead bodies that she had ever seen. She was so mature, so far ahead of even he had been at her age, that Beckett had a hard time accepting that she was only a first-year medical student.

Well, he thought, remembering the day when he had been exposed to his first corpse, *better now with me than in front of classmates.*

He took a deep breath.

"Suze, if it's too much..." he let his sentence trail off.

She shook her head.

"No, it's fine. I want to help."

"Did you find anything on the Internet about the images? Anything at all?"

Suzan turned then, and Beckett was surprised by the fire in her eyes. When he had seen his first body he had been anxious, nervous, and a little queasy. Suzan, on the other hand, seemed... *determined.*

"I found something... there's a bulletin board on a medical resource site, and a couple of months back someone started asking questions about Moorfield's forensic pathology course. At first, I didn't think much of it, but then..." she shrugged and let her sentence trail off.

"Then what?"

She looked away.

"Nothing. It's just the timing seemed too coincidental, is all."

Beckett instantly knew that she was lying; the steel had gone out of her eyes.

The question was, *why?*

Beckett stared at her for a moment, unsure of how to proceed. He felt the knot in his gut again, but this time the message was clear: *you shouldn't get her involved. She's too young, too naive.*

"You okay?"

Beckett shook the thoughts from his head and smiled.

Just a new set of eyes, a new perspective. That's all. Then she can go back to her normal life.

"Yeah, I'm fine. Now look, I don't want you to be embarrassed if you get sick around the bodies. And if you at all feel uncomfortable, we can just shut this down, alright?"

Suzan stared at him strangely, and he quickly realized that the reason for the look was his out of character response.

"Of course, you can always be an engineer, instead of a doctor. I mean, you'd probably look good in a tall striped hat."

Suzan smirked, then turned and without hesitation, pulled the sheet off of Trevor Gobbets's body.

Chapter 41

IT AMAZED DRAKE HOW easily he slipped back into detective mode and how comfortable he felt in doing so.

Do you miss it?

Maybe...

His first stop was the location of Dr. Edison Larringer's death. He was the key—unlike the others who had been selected based on the fact that no one would question their suicides, Eddie had been murdered because of the photographs he had stolen from Beckett's desk. That much was obvious, but the real question was, why were the photographs placed on Beckett's desk in the first place?

To answer that question, Drake needed to learn a little more about the black sheep of the five victims.

Although Drake was no longer a police officer, and could no longer flash the detective shield—like that did him much good in the past, anyway—Screech had made up some fancy Private Investigator business cards that he hoped were sufficient to get him in the door.

529 3rd Ave was a run-down apartment building not far from NYU Medical Center. Drake took a deep breath and walked up to the cracked concrete steps to the door, and then rapped his knuckles briskly off the painted surface.

As he waited for someone to answer, he leaned away from the house, looking upward, noting that there was a window roughly twelve feet up. He was imagining what it would take for someone to scale the brick wall and pry that window open, when the door swung wide.

A young girl in her early twenties sporting a gray tracksuit stood in the doorway. Her eyes were red and her cheeks chaffed from tears.

"Hello?" she asked with a sniff.

Drake cleared his throat and then reached into his pocket and withdrew a business card.

"My name is Damien Drake," he said, holding the card out to her. Her eyes narrowed in suspicion, but she took the card without hesitation. "I have a few questions I wanted to ask you about someone who lived here."

"Eddie," she said softly, her eyes still locked on the card. "You're here about Eddie."

Drake nodded.

"Yes. Did you know him?"

Her eyes shot up.

"Of course I knew him," she snapped. "I lived with him."

"I'm very sorry for—"

"Save it," she said. "If one more person says I'm sorry for your loss, I'm going to scream."

The woman, apparently having finished reading the card, held it out to him.

Drake frowned, thinking that this was going to be a bust.

"Keep it, and if you—"

"Do you think Eddie committed suicide?" she asked suddenly.

Drake opened his mouth to answer, but was interrupted by a male voice coming from somewhere within the apartment complex.

"Steff? You okay? Who's at the door?"

The girl in the track suit turned her head toward a door off to the right.

"I'm fine. I got it!"

When she turned back, her expression had hardened.

"Well, do you?"

Drake shook his head.

"No, I don't. Which is why I'm here."

She stared at him for several uncomfortable seconds, clearly sizing him up.

"Ok," she said at last, stepping off to one side. "Then come in."

***

"He wouldn't commit suicide. No matter how bad things got, he wouldn't do *that*. There's just no way," the woman, who had introduced herself as Stephanie—Steff—Morgan said. She placed a cup of hot coffee down in front of Drake and then took a seat across from him, cradling her own mug in both hands.

"I hate to be insensitive, but how do you know? I mean, I get that you lived together, but were you close?"

Steff looked away for a moment, and then lowered her voice.

"We were close," she said, her eyes returning to him.

Drake knew better than to push for a deeper explanation; he could read between the lines.

"And how—"

The sound of a person approaching from behind drew his attention. A man with a shaved head, wearing an NYU sweatshirt entered the kitchen. He had a scar on his lip and another above his left eye, and Drake noted several tattoos peeking out from the wrists of the sweatshirt.

"Who are you?" the man asked suspiciously.

Drake stood and offered his hand.

"Damien Drake. I'm a private investigator."

The man looked at his hand with something akin to disgust on his face. He didn't shake it.

"A private investigator? What do you want?"

Drake lowered his hand.

"I just wanted to ask Steff, and maybe you, about Eddie. I just have a few questions, is all."

The man's eyes narrowed, which made the scar above his eye jut out.

"Why? The police have already been here… what? Five times? Six? Eddie offed himself, plain and simple."

"No, it wasn't, Jake. It wasn't a suicide," Steff interrupted.

"No? And how would you know that, Steff? You fucking clairvoyant now?"

She lowered her eyes.

"I just do," she answered softly.

The man that Steff had called Jake walked by them and went to the fridge, where he pulled out a carton of milk. He unscrewed the top and took a swig.

"Yeah right, the dude hung himself. The police say it's suicide, so why can't you just accept it? You an expert? Know more than they do?"

Steff said nothing.

"Hey, I'm talking to you."

Drake observed this scene in silence. It was one that he was unfortunately familiar with.

Jake and Steff were dating, and if he didn't hit her yet, he would start soon. Drake just wasn't sure how Eddie fit into this mix.

Jake took another gulp of milk before putting the container back in the fridge.

"I just… I just know he wouldn't," Steff answered at last.

Jake laughed.

"Dude, he was flunking out. You saw him, he was losing it. Some people just can't handle the pressure, you know? Darwin 'n all that. Survival of the fittest."

This seemed to strike a nerve with Steff.

"Oh, and you know pressure, Jake? Now *you're* the expert? You haven't had to work a day in your life… mommy and daddy just pay for everything. Paid to get you into school, pay to get you out of trouble. You know nothing about pressure. Eddie was a good man, and he worked hard. Sure he was nervous about his exams, but who isn't? I'll say it again, there's no way he committed suicide."

Jake took a step forward.

"You watch your mouth," he threatened through clenched teeth.

And that's enough of that.

Drake got to his feet and moved between them.

"Why don't you calm down, Jake. I can see—"

Jake's eyes turned on him.

"I got an idea: why don't you mind your fucking business, rent-a-cop? What the fuck you doing here, anyway?" the man took a step toward him when he said this, but Drake didn't back down.

"I told you, I'm just here to ask a few questions, that's all. I don't want any trouble."

Jake took another step forward, and in his periphery, Drake saw his the man's hands ball into fists.

"Question period is over, dumb ass. Take a hike."

Drake felt his blood pressure rise.

Do it, punk. Throw a punch. I dare you.

Jake must have seen something in his face, as although he must have had three inches and at least ten pounds on Drake, he was the one who backed away.

"We don't want to talk to you," he said.

Drake turned back to Steff. All of a sudden her cup of coffee was incredibly interesting to her.

"Please, just go," she said in a quiet voice.

Drake nodded, gave one more searing glance at Jake then made his way to the door.

"If you can think of anything that might help, please give me a call," he said over his shoulder.

He grabbed the door and pulled it wide.

"Don't hold your breath," Jake yelled after him. "Or maybe you should hold your breath, you fucking asshole. Or better yet, get a rope and off yourself like Eddie did."

Chapter 42

"Ashes," Suzan said. At first, Beckett thought that she was speaking to herself. But when she repeated the word, he took notice.

"Ashes? What do you mean, ashes?"

Beckett moved beside her as she inspected Gerald Leblanc, the male escort who had been shot in the face. It took him a moment to realize that she wasn't staring at his mangled head. Instead, she was staring at the hollow of his throat.

"Look? See there?" she pointed at a gray smudge. "When I was younger my dad used to take me to church, and on Good Friday, the priest would wipe this soot on my forehead. It looked like this—obviously, this isn't in the shape of a cross, but it sure looks the same."

Beckett frowned.

"Where?" He leaned closer to the body to get a better look. There did appear to be a smudge where she had indicated, but had Suzan not said anything, he would have passed it off as dirt, or a mark that one of the CSU boys had left behind when they had removed the body from the scene. "Just looks like dirt to me."

Suzan acknowledged his comment, and then moved to the body of Martin Dean, the man who had apparently slit his wrists in the bathtub.

"Except it's on every single one of them," she said with a hint of pride in her voice.

"Seriously?"

Suzan moved up to Trevor's body next.

"See? There's another one on his left shoulder."

Beckett squinted.

It was there, just as she said. Another quarter-sized gray smudge.

"I also found one on the, uh, the doctor. Nothing on the drowned woman, but she was submerged, so…"

Beckett was flabbergasted.

How the hell did I miss this?

"Gimme one sec," he said, and without another word, he left the room. A minute later he returned with a bespectacled CSU tech in tow.

"Jeff, I want you to take some samples from all of the marks that Suzan shows you. I want a complete analysis, fingerprints, DNA, mass spec, etc. Can you do that?"

Jeff looked at Beckett as if he had three heads.

"These are… what are these bodies doing here? Aren't these the sui—"

Beckett gently guided him toward the first body.

"Just take the samples, okay? And I want the results today. The sooner, the better," he instructed. "Okay, Jeff?"

The man's thin lips pressed together.

"My name is Seb."

Beckett nodded.

"Good. That's a yes then."

Chapter 43

"No, no, no," Officer Steve Dunbar said when Chase opened the door to the dimly lit room tucked into the basement of 62nd precinct.

Just one look at her, and it was clear that he had his mind made up.

"Good afternoon to you too, Dunbar," Chase said, stepping inside. She looked around quickly and noted that aside from the myriad of computer equipment, the place was empty. On one desk was a coffee mug, but the other desk, the one with the leather-backed ergonomic chair tucked beneath, was completely bare.

Dunbar swiped a lock of blond hair from his forehead.

"Detective Adams, it's great to see you, but I'm on vacation."

Chase's eyes narrowed.

"Vacation? What do you mean, vacation?" she stepped deeper into the room—officially marked as *Records*, even though every officer knew it as the unofficial computer hub for the entire precinct—the smell of hot metal filled her nostrils.

Officer Dunbar looked around nervously, then reached for her. Confused, Chase allowed herself to be pulled behind a metal shelf filled with black binders.

"Adams, I can't even be seen talking to you."

"What? Why not?"

"Rhodes came down here earlier, told me that under no circumstances was I to help you out with any cold cases. I'm supposed to inform him if you ask me to do anything, even if it's related to the home invasion on Forty-Third Street. He came right after you asked me to look up the med students.

Shit, you so much as cough in my direction and I'm supposed to call him on his cell phone. You should have seen his face..."

In her mind, she saw Rhodes's face turning red, his eyes wide behind his glasses, his Adam's apple bobbing.

It was frightening how vivid the image was.

"Dunbar," she said softly, "I need your help."

"Yeah, I know. But I can't. Shit, the last time... with the Butterfly Killer? I almost lost my job, Chase," he held his finger and thumb less than an inch apart. "Seriously, I was this close."

Chase tried not to let the surprise show in her face. She knew that Drake had gone to great lengths to protect her, but she hadn't thought about the implications for others.

Like Officer Dunbar, who had been instrumental in them getting the information they needed to connect the murders, and to lead them to Dr. Mark Kruk.

"I didn't know," she said simply. *If I had known*, was on the tip of her tongue, but she resisted the urge to say it.

If she had known... then what? Would she have protected Dunbar when she was promoted to Detective First Grade, if that would mean going against Rhodes? Would she do that?

Chase wanted to think that she would, but wasn't positive. And, besides, she hadn't known, so there was no point losing sleep over what she might have done.

Coulda, woulda, shoulda.

"I'm sorry about what happened to you, Dunbar. But that doesn't change anything. I need your help, again."

Dunbar looked at her with round eyes.

Please, his expression said, *don't ask me to do this.*

But with all due respect to Officer Dunbar, finding the ruthless killer who had already murdered five people and was destined to kill at least three more before he was done, was more important than his job.

Than any of their jobs, hers included.

"Dunbar, please. There's a murderer out there, and he's not going to stop until we catch him."

Officer Dunbar closed his eyes and he mumbled something that she didn't pick up. With a heavy sigh, he looked at her again.

"Fine… tell me exactly what you need, and make it quick."

Chapter 44

Suzan Cuthbert rubbed her eyes and yawned.

How long has it been since I've slept? She thought. *Twenty-four hours? Thirty-six?*

She had fallen asleep at Beckett's computer last night while searching for information on the images from the forensic pathology course, but she couldn't have been out for more than a half hour.

Forty minutes, tops.

What had started as simply auditing Beckett's course, had quickly ballooned into something bigger, something more important. Something so important that it meant more to her than going to class, which was exactly where she should be right now.

Except she wasn't in class. Suzan had left the morgue with a strange lightheartedness, something that she tried desperately to convince herself was a result of inhaling formalin in the morgue rather than the sight of five dead bodies. Instead of class, she headed back to Beckett's office, using the key that he had loaned her, knowing that he would be teaching for the next hour or so. And now she sat, exhausted, hungry, and determined, hunched over Beckett's computer, logging in with the man's NYU credentials, which he had also provided her.

Suzan immediately loaded the bulletin board on which she had first noticed the strange questions regarding the forensic pathology course. She was about to scroll down to the newest post, when she noticed that the icon of the envelope near the top of the screen had turned red.

Curious, Suzan clicked on it, and a new message appeared onscreen.

Are you interested in pathology?

Suzan's heart started to thrum in her chest. When she read the handle of the person who had sent the message, a thin sheen of sweat formed on her forehead.

Arsonist514.

She swallowed hard.

Arsonist514 had been the name of the person posting about forensic pathology.

The same person who had responded to Eddie's posts about wanting help with the exam.

Should I tell Beckett? Chase?

Suzan stared at the message for so long that she started to get tunnel vision.

"No," she said out loud. The sound was loud in the confined space that was Beckett's office, and it startled her.

If she told either of them, she knew what they would do. They would do exactly the same thing her dad would have done had he still been alive.

They would tell her to go home, to forget all about this.

They would try to protect her.

Only Suzan didn't want protection; she wanted to catch a killer. Besides, they couldn't protect anyone, not really.

Had they protected dad? Made sure that he comes home from work to tuck me in?

"No," she said again, her voice hitching. Gritting her teeth, she leaned forward and hit the reply button.

Chapter 45

"**Hey Drake, it's Screech,**" the voice on the other end of the line said.

Drake stepped into his Crown Vic and shut the door.

"Yeah, what's up?"

"Just wondering if you're coming in this afternoon."

There was a hint of nervousness in his partner's voice, which seemed out of place.

"Why? What's going on? You find out anything about the murders?" Drake asked as he put the keys in the ignition and the Vic roared to life.

"No, not that. I'm still looking…"

"Then? What is it?" he cast a look back toward the door of 529 3rd Ave, hoping that Steff would come out and flag him down.

It remained closed.

"It's—well, I was putting in more cameras for the GILFs that visited this morning, and I switched over to Mrs. Armatridge's feed by accident," Screech paused, and Drake started driving.

"And? Screech, spit it out, man. I don't have time for this."

"Fuck, sorry. It's just I saw the maid, uh, Consuela or whatever her name is, and she was helping Mr. Armatridge to bed."

"Yeah, so?"

"So, she didn't just put him to bed," Screech said hesitantly, "but she went to bed *with* him."

Drake wasn't sure he had heard right. A horn honked, and he realized that with his attention elsewhere he had drifted into the opposing lane.

He righted the vehicle.

"*With* him? Like, *with* him?"

"With him," Screech confirmed.

"Jesus, he must be what, like eighty?"

"At least."

Drake put his blinker on and turned away from the heart of the city, taking a winding road that was flanked by large berms of freshly cut grass.

"Well?" Screech asked. "What do you want me to do?"

Drake thought about it for a moment.

"Do we record it?"

"Yep, everything is backed up in the cloud."

Drake instinctively turned his eyes upward, staring at the setting sun. He still couldn't get used to the idea of information being stored in a cloud, digital or celestial.

"Alright, then you don't have to do anything. Just make sure you don't lose the recording. I'll speak to Mrs. Armatridge in the morning. In the meantime, I need something to go on with the pathology murders, Screech. Eddie's roommates were a dead end. Get me something."

He thought about Eddie, about how nervous he had looked when he had come to see him, the way his eyes had darted about like a possum rising from the earth after the rain.

If I had only…

He shook his head and turned onto another street, the Manhattan skyscape shrinking in the distance.

"Hey Drake, you okay? You sound… *different*."

"Fine," he grumbled. "Just see what you can find, okay?"

"Alrighty. I'm on it, boss."

Drake grimaced at the use of the word; it was the same term that he had used jokingly with Chase when they had been working the Butterfly Killer case.

Do you miss it? Screech had asked.

Drake had said no, that the money was good in PI, that he was moving on, that he had given up on the life that had taken so much from him.

But now, feeling the blood coursing through his veins with renewed vigor, he realized that it had been a lie. This whole time, he had been lying to everyone.

The worst part was that he had been lying to himself.

With a heavy sigh, Drake turned his head to the iron archway over the worn dirt path that marked the entrance to Fallen Heights Cemetery.

Then he stepped out into the sun.

***

Drake slumped into the front seat of his car and then wiped the tears from his eyes.

He had hoped that coming here, that visiting Clay's grave would give him some insight into the murders, help him think like Clay had, but it had been a fool's errand.

The only thing that coming here had given him was a bad case of memories.

His phone buzzed in his pocket and he pulled it out, clearing his throat before answering.

"Screech? Did you find something?"

It seemed impossible, given that they had spoken less than an hour ago, but up until a week ago the idea of having miniature cameras set up and transmit live, high-quality video directly to his cell phone had seemed like science fiction, as well.

The only response was heavy breathing.

Drake sat up straight.

"Screech? Everything okay?"

"It's… it's Steff."

Drake's eyes narrowed, and he thought about the way that Jake had spoken to her, to both of them.

He better not have hit her.

"Steff, everything okay?"

"I don't—I don't have much time. He'll be back soon, and he doesn't want me talking to you."

"Who? Who doesn't—"

"Jake. Can we meet? I don't have much time."

Drake slammed the car into drive.

"Patty's Diner. You know it?"

There was a short pause.

"I can find it."

Drake's foot jammed down hard on the gas pedal and his Crown Vic leaped forward.

"Good, I'll meet you there in twenty," he said as he sped back toward the city.

Chapter 46

Kenneth Smith took a long pull on his cigar, admiring the way the tendrils of smoke wrapped around the glowing end.

"Raul? Any update on the numbers?"

Raul stepped around the front of his chair, a silver tray with a bottle of Johnny Walker Blue and a single glass resting on the top in his outstretched hands.

"You are still ahead by three points on most polls," a stone-faced Raul said in his thick Spanish accent.

As Raul poured two fingers of whiskey and set the glass on the table beside Ken, he took another drag of his cigar.

"But Dr. Hammond still has a lead in all districts around NYU. Have I got that right?"

"*Jes*, sir."

Ken took a sip of whiskey. After what had happened to Thomas, he had thought that his mayorship was all but a given. But while he had garnered some—*most*—of the sympathy vote, and he had the backing of the NYPD, a doctor with the impeccable record that Dr. Hammond possessed proved to be a tougher challenge than expected.

Impeccable record… no one is that clean.

Ken thought back to his conversation with Damien Drake all those months ago and realized that he was still missing someone on his staff with the man's particular skill set.

All-in-all, he was pleased with the way that things worked out in the wake of the Butterfly Killer. Rhodes had played his role well; he had forced Drake out of the force, just as Ken had intended. But then something strange happened.

Drake didn't take the bait; he never came knocking on Ken's door, asking to take him up on his offer as he had expected, as he had planned.

Raul had done some recon and had found out that Drake was now running a small PI firm in the East end of the city.

He knew Drake, and people like him. He had come across dozens of iterations during his time as a litigator. People like Drake just couldn't stay away. They could try, and by all accounts, Drake had given it a valiant effort, but it was only a matter of time before everything else in his life seemed inconsequential.

The man had been marked at birth; marked to track down the most villainous, immoral members of society. And nothing could temper that uncompromising urge.

And yet Ken had never expected it to go this far, had never thought that he had to enact part two of his plan.

Ken finished his whiskey and indicated for Raul to pour him another glass.

Six months until election day.

And when that day came, he wanted Damien Drake at his side.

"You okay, sir?" Raul asked, concern in his voice.

Ken took a drag from his cigar, once again watching the hypnotic way the smoke curled and wrapped itself around the air before dissipating.

"Fine," he said. "I'm fine."

He needed Drake by his side, and it was only a matter of time before he had him. Because what Ken Smith wanted, Ken Smith got. And that was how *he* was wired.

Chapter 47

SCREECH CRACKED HIS KNUCKLES then he took a deep breath and attacked his keyboard, typing with such speed that his fingers became a blur.

He was still in shock that Drake had gone ahead and offered him half of Triple D. A week ago, Screech had considered his position, and honestly, the PI firm as a whole, a stopgap measure. After all, before Mrs. Armatridge, things had been going very, very slowly. Drake wasn't well liked by the NYPD, and although the idea of having an ex-NYPD detective as a PI was appealing to most, clients were still hesitant. People knew Drake, and their knowledge was based on what the media published, which wasn't favorable.

But then Mrs. Armatridge had shown up, seemingly out of nowhere, and all of a sudden things had changed.

Which was fine by Screech. He wasn't one to question the karma of the cosmos; quite the contrary. He went with the flow. And if solving these murders managed to get Drake back in the NYPD and the public's good graces, then that would only serve to increase the number of Mrs. Armatridge-types that came in through the door.

But it was more than that; no moral justice warrior was Screech, and yet there was something to be said for being part of a team that took a murder of the street. That had to be worth more than helping old bitties put a maid in jail for stealing silverware.

Much more.

Screech spent the next half hour looking into the forensic pathology course notes, focusing on their availability online. But when this brought up no leads, he took a short break to crush a Mountain Dew and reconsider.

What had Chase and Drake said? That the young doctor was key. He was the odd man out, the one that didn't quite fit with the drifters and those shunned by society that had turned up dead.

When Screech turned back to his computer, he changed his approach. Instead of looking into the pathology course, he started to read about the students, about the lives that medical students and residents lived.

And then, after nearly an hour of searching, he came across something that he thought interesting. It wasn't an article about NYU medical students, but an article in the Montreal Gazette about McGill University, a prestigious university in Montreal, Quebec. In explicit terms, the article outlined the transgressions of the medical staff, their mistreatment of the students, about how their medical school license was in jeopardy as a result of their actions. It didn't appear to be the case of the students being spoiled brats, either. There were reports of young doctors who weren't allowed to go to the bathroom for hours on end for fear of being berated in front of their peers, about forty-hour shifts without breaks. All of this had culminated with a patient being prescribed a contraindicated medication that put the poor schlep in a coma for more than a week.

Screech leaned back again, letting this all sink in.

"Huh," he said, grateful that his route of post-secondary education, as short as it had been, had taken him into computer engineering and not medicine. Groaning, Screech stood and made his way to the fridge, withdrawing the last Mountain Dew. He popped the top, waited for the fizz to die down, then returned to his chair.

On a whim, he typed the name of the doctor who had created the forensic pathology slides, Dr. Tracey Moorfield.

As expected, nothing interesting came to the fore. But when he combined her name with 'academic misconduct' he got a hit.

Just a single article, published more than two decades ago.

Swishing the citrusy liquid around in his mouth, Screech rubbed his eyes, then started to read.

Chapter 48

THERE WAS SOMETHING ABOUT Broomhilda's presence in Patty's Diner that felt oddly comfortable to Drake, that felt normal.

"Coffee, please," he said when she came over to serve him. While he had recognized her immediately, her flat expression suggested that she had no idea who he was. Drake supposed that was a good thing, although he wasn't entirely sure. "And Key Lime pie, if it's fresh."

The woman grunted then turned back toward the kitchen.

A moment later, the door opened, and Drake felt his breath come more quickly. He pictured Ivan Meitzer coming through the door, a dark hood pulled over his head, a bulge in his chest where he kept the envelope full of cash.

But it wasn't Ivan who entered Patty's Diner, but a woman. Like Ivan, however, she had the hood of her sweatshirt over her head, shrouding her face in shadows.

"Steff?" he said just loud enough for her to hear. "Over here."

The woman turned to face him and then hurried to the booth.

"I don't have much time," she said. Drake tried to lean down to get a better look at her face, but she tucked her chin, hiding her features.

"What's going on, Steff?" he asked with concern.

She ignored the comment.

"There is no way that Eddie committed suicide. Sure, he was struggling, but all of his friends were struggling, too. Based on everything that he told me, Dr. Campbell is tough."

Drake considered this for a moment, trying to picture his friend with the spiky hair, the wide smile, doing his best Mussolini impression at the front of the classroom.

But no matter how hard he tried, he just couldn't get the image to stick.

"He said... he said he had found something, something about the forensic pathology course that had scared him."

Drake nodded and for a brief moment, he debated telling the girl that Eddie had come to see him with the same concerns, before deciding against it. He didn't want to bias her; he was here to listen to what she had to say, and that was all. That was his role in this.

For now.

"Did he say anything else? Anything that might help find the bastard who did this to him?"

Steff tilted her head backward, just enough for Drake to make out her chin and lower lip. He thought he caught sight the beginnings of a bruise at the corner of her mouth, and his mind turned to Jake back in the kitchen.

He's started hitting her.

Drake hated abusive boyfriends and spouses nearly as much as he hated the murderers he had spent the better part of a decade chasing.

"Eddie told me that he was looking for a tutor online and he came across a bulletin board. Someone reached out to him, and told him that he had the answers to the upcoming final exam."

"Did he say anything about this guy? Did he go and meet him?"

Steff shook her head and as she did, her hood slipped backward, revealing a nasty welt below her right eye.

"He just said that the man somehow obtained the answers, that's all."

"Did he give a name? A description? Anything to go on?"

Steff chewed her lip again.

"The only thing that he told me was the man's handle on the bulletin board."

"And? What was it?"

Steff leaned forward and was about to say something, when her phone buzzed. With a trembling hand, she pulled it from her pocket and stared at the glowing screen, her eyes going wide.

"Shit. He's looking for me." Steff leaped to her feet. "I have to go."

Drake stood as well. He reached for her, but she cowered away from him.

"I'm sorry, I have to go. I can't..." she let her sentence trail off.

"Don't go back to him, Steff," Drake said quickly. "I've seen people like him, and the abuse... it's not going to stop. It's only going to get worse. Don't go back to him."

Steff started toward the door, her pace frantic now.

"I'm sorry, I just can't. I have to go."

She was nearly at the door by the time Drake managed to slide out of the booth.

"Wait! Steff, *wait!*"

But she didn't wait; instead, she pulled the door wide so violently that the small metal bell above the door almost flew off the hook.

Drake, aware that everyone in the diner was now looking at him, but not caring, shouted, "What was the handle, Steff? What was the man's handle?"

Steff paused and then turned back.

"Arson, something or other," she said, then added, "I'm sorry."

With that, she was gone.

Drake stood in the center of the diner as he watched her go, stunned by what she had told him.

Someone placed a hand on his shoulder and he jumped. He whipped around and found himself staring at Broomhilda's weathered face.

"You still want your Key Lime pie?"

Chapter 49

CHASE TAPPED HER PEN on her desk, filling her office with a tinny drumroll. Every few minutes her eyes flicked over to the other desk, before frowning when it remained empty. She remembered Drake sitting there, across from her, swearing as he tried to figure out how to get the department computer system to work.

After Drake had resigned, Rhodes had promoted her, but while he had promised to get her a new partner, there didn't seem to be any movement on that front.

It got lonely inside her own head; she missed someone with the grace of a bull to occupy her thoughts.

She missed Drake.

It hadn't occurred to her before, but now that they were working together again, albeit on an informal basis, it was something that she couldn't ignore.

And she saw it in his eyes, too; *he* missed her—if not her, then at least the job.

Tap, tap, tap, tap, went her pen.

Focus, Chase.

But she couldn't focus. This wasn't like any other case that she had been a part of during her career—in Seattle or in NYC. She was working to find a killer whom no one but her party of misfits thought existed.

But maybe... maybe that's our edge, she thought suddenly. *Nobody knows that we're looking for him, not even the killer.*

Chase made a *hmph* sound as she considered this.

Nobody knows that we're looking for a killer...

Except that wasn't quite true. Dr. Edison knew that something was up. And he had ended up dead.

Everyone else was a drifter, a nobody.

It was clear that their killer preferred to take out the lower rungs of society, but wasn't afraid to climb up that ladder if someone threatened to put them in the limelight. If someone got close, he wouldn't hesitate to make them part of his macabre re-enactments, no matter who it was.

Chase tried to put the puzzle pieces together in her head, but this got her nowhere.

She picked up her phone and hit redial.

"Dunbar? Its Chase. You got anything yet?"

"Hold on a sec," Dunbar whispered. She heard him shuffling and then the sound of a door closing. "Chase? Geez, you have to stop calling me every ten minutes. People are going to get suspicious."

Chase grimaced.

"Yeah, sorry. You got anything for me?"

"No, nothing. I have to… well, I told you. I have to be careful where I look. If Rhodes does a simple back search, he's gonna figure out what I've been doing."

"'Kay. Just let me know as soon as you find something— anything. Anything in Dr. Edison Larringer's background that is interesting, okay? Shit, you know what? If you find *anything* about Eddie, let me know."

"Will do," Dunbar said before signing off.

Chase hung up the phone and raised her eyes to the other desk, ready to say something to Drake, before remembering that it was still empty.

Tap, tap, tap.

Eddie got close, and that's why he ended up dead, Chase thought. *And if he got close, then so can I. It's just a matter of retracing his steps, starting with where he had found the photographs, starting with Beckett's office.*

Chase stood and started to put on her trench coat when her phone buzzed on her desk. She grabbed it and answered with one arm still hanging out of her jacket.

"Dunbar? You find anything?"

"Uh, Detective Adams? It's Detective Yasiv."

"Oh, shit, sorry. What's up?"

"Well, we've got a strange situation here. There's been an accident; a tow truck driver's dead."

Chase's eyes immediately narrowed and she sat at her desk, instinctively opening the folder of photographs from the forensic pathology course.

Please, not another one.

"Yeah? And why is it strange? How'd he die?"

Chase heard Henry Yasiv swallow hard.

"It looks like... it looks like he was electrocuted. I mean, the cables are still hooked up to his tow truck battery, but the strange thing is, there's no other car on the scene. I mean, there's *nothing* out here but weeds and allergies. Nothing— Chase? You still there?"

Chase knew that Detective Yasiv was speaking to her, but she wasn't hearing any of his words.

Instead, her eyes were locked on the sixth photograph from the exam.

The one that showed a man with a silver-dollar-sized burn mark on his neck, and another on his shoulder.

There was a single word printed on the top of the image: ELECTROCUTION.

Their killer had struck again. Only this time, it looked like he got sloppy.

Chapter 50

SUZAN TUCKED HER CHIN into her coat for warmth and glanced around. Her heart was beating hard in her chest, and it was all she could do to resist the urge to sprint back to her car and get the hell out of here.

It was dumb meeting the man who went by Arsonist514 — no, dumb was too weak a word for it. Meeting him was perhaps one of the stupidest things that she had ever done. But she had taken precautions.

Suzan was standing on the corner of a busy intersection, with dozens of people milling about, coming to or going from work. It was close to five in the afternoon, and the corner that they had chosen to meet was so busy that she had to fight to avoid being swept away with the crowd.

Her hand slipped into her jacket pocket, confirming for the tenth or eleventh time that the can of pepper spray was still in there.

In there, with the cap off. In her other hand, she held her cell phone, pretending to be scrolling through text messages, while in reality, she had the camera at the ready to snap a pic of the man who called himself Arsonist514.

She wasn't positive that he was the killer—had she been, there was no way in hell she would have agreed to meet him—and nothing other than his keen interest in the forensic pathology course alluded to any involvement in the crimes at all.

But the feeling in her gut told her that if he wasn't the killer, then he knew who was.

Are you interested in pathology? The message had read. Suzan's reply had been equally as simple and cryptic: *Keen interest; need answers.*

When she typed that message, she had been someone else; or, at least, she had *tried* to be someone else.

Suzan put herself in Dr. Larringer's shoes, try to act as he had, a frantic student on the verge of failing his courses, desperate for anything that might help him get the edge he needed to succeed.

From there, things had snowballed quickly, more quickly than she had hoped, and now, before she had a chance to really think about what was happening, she had agreed to meet the man.

Suzan's eyes darted around, trying to tease the man out from the crowd, even though he hadn't even given so much as a hint of what he looked like.

Someone bumped her arm, and she yelped. Whipping around, she started to pull the pepper spray from her pocket.

"Excuse me," a tall man in a suit muttered as he hurried past.

Suzan took a deep breath and offered a tense smile in return.

All she wanted to do was snap a pic, then head back to see Beckett and Chase. To impress them with what she had done. Sure, they might be upset at her, but when they saw that she had an actual photograph of someone who might be involved, then they would have no choice but to thank her.

But when the sun progressed from half-mast to nearly sunk, Suzan's excitement waned with pathetic fallacy.

He's not coming, she thought with dismay. *He's not coming. It was just a thirteen-year-old fat kid hiding behind a computer screen, getting his jollies by sending her on a wild goose chase.*

And yet Suzan continued to wait. Even as the crowds began to thin, and the thin veil of comfort that they afforded her began to wash away, she waited.

When it turned seven, Suzan looked down at her cell phone.

With a sigh, she scrolled to Beckett's number.

It rang three times before going to the machine.

"You have reached the mailbox of Dr. Beckett Campbell. If you're hearing this message, you're one of the lucky few who have my number. Congrats. And if it's you—you know who you are—asking about the damn rash again, I told you a thousand times: add kerosene and scrub it with a wire brush. If it's you, mom, I won't be home for dinner."

Suzan rolled her eyes and waited for the beep before leaving her message.

"Beckett, it's Suzan. I've found something online. Give me a shout when you get this."

Then she hung up and made her way back to her car. Part of her was disappointed that Arsonist514 hadn't shown up, but part of her was also relieved.

"This was stupid," she said to herself as she got into her car. And then, for some reason, she laughed.

It was a nervous giggle, one that she didn't recognize. But more surprising than this sound was what came next: the tears.

Along with this unexpected deluge of emotion were thoughts of her dad, of the way he used to give her noogies even though she hated them.

"Stop it," she admonished herself between sobs. "Just fucking stop it, Suzan. Grow up. He's gone, and catching this guy won't bring him back."

She wiped the tears from her face and then put the keys in the ignition. With a sniff, she started her car.

Suzan Cuthbert reached for the gear shift, intending to put the car into drive when she felt something cold and sharp touch the side of her bare neck.

She inhaled sharply.

"So you're interested in pathology?" a gruff voice from the backseat said and Suzan felt her entire body go numb.

Part IV – Homicide

Chapter 51

IT HAD BEEN A while since Drake had spent so much time investigating a case… a *real* case. And it was wearing on him. He could feel his body trembling slightly as exhaustion began to take hold.

Six months at Triple D had made him soft.

With a sigh, his eyes closed and it took a deliberate effort to open them again.

Okay, maybe not soft.

Softer.

And despite the effort he had put in, he was still no closer to finding the killer. He had, however, witnessed domestic abuse and all of its disgusting inevitability. That was something he intended to deal with. In time, he would teach the prick Jake that he wasn't as tough as he thought.

Drake pulled his leaden limbs from his Crown Vic and made his way to the front door of Triple D. He was surprised to find it unlocked, and even more surprised to find Screech inside, his face illuminated by the artificial glow from his computer screen.

"Screech? What are you still doing here?"

The man whipped around, and the way he blinked rapidly and his hands twitched, Drake knew that he was hopped up on caffeine or maybe even something stronger.

"Working, Drake, my man. Working. Dug up some shit that might help." Even the man's speech was rapid, clipped.

Drake suddenly felt awake again, the last vestiges of adrenaline leaking from his adrenals and flooding his system. He strode into the reception area, closing the door behind him.

"What did you find?"

"I found—"

But Drake heard a sound from his office and peered over Screech's shoulder.

The door to his office stood ajar.

"Someone's here?" he whispered. "Please tell me it's not Mrs. Armatridge. I can't deal with her right now."

Screech shook his head and was about to answer when a familiar voice spoke from within his office.

"Honey? That you? Dinner better be ready in ten. And none of that microwaved crap again."

Drake smiled a weary smile.

It was Beckett.

"Get your ass in here!" his friend hollered.

Drake turned to Screech.

"I thought your job was to keep the riff-raff out," he said. Screech just shrugged. "Alright, let's all meet in my office — you can tell me what you've found in there."

Beckett was sitting behind his desk, his feet up. In his hand was a glass of scotch. He looked at it, swirled the liquid, and then took a sip.

"Not bad, not bad," he glanced up at Drake. "Oh, I took one of those hefty checks. You know — for my cut."

"Very funny," Drake said, taking a seat across from Beckett. Screech sat beside him. "Let's get a move on here. I'm tired as hell."

The jovial expression slid off Beckett's face.

"Aren't we all. All right, Screech, why don't you go first. Tell us what you've got."

Screech cleared his throat and Drake turned to face him.

"Yeah, so I was following up on our doctor friend, Eddie, based on the fact that he's the odd one out. I couldn't really find anything about him—seemed like just a normal guy, lots of friends, lots of stress… over the last six months, however, he started to post less to his Facebook and Twitter feeds. I'm guessing he was either getting depressed or just had no time for it anymore. Anyways, I kept on looking, only this time I searched the 'net and found two things of interest: one, the website that Eddie was posting on, and, two, something about Dr. Moorfield. Which do you want to hear first?"

Drake glanced over at Beckett, then at the same time, they both said, "The website."

Screech gave them a look.

"Okay, well, website it is. Want me to show you the transcript?"

"Transcript? Jesus, just tell us what you found, Screech. And calm the hell down."

The man swiped sweat from his forehead, then ran his fingers through his curly hair.

"Yes, right. Anyways, so apparently, Eddie was online asking questions about the test? Some sort of bulletin board for doctors and students. Anyways, there was nothing interesting until a few months ago when this one guy shows up, starts answering his questions about the test, saying he has the photographs from the exam."

Screech paused for effect, and Drake impatiently waved a hand, urging him to continue.

"And?"

Screech shrugged.

"That's it. I mean, the guy seemed to know a lot about the test, but nothing came of it."

"Okay, Jacques Cousteau, you manage to track him down? Find out who this mystery man is?" Beckett asked.

Screech shook his head.

"Nope. He fell silent after a couple of exchanges. But then…"

"Then what?"

"Then he popped up again just yesterday—someone had revived the old thread."

"And there's no way you can find out who it is? Anything about him?" Drake asked.

"I tried tracing his IP address, but it just pinged all over Southeast Asia."

Drake frowned and considered asking what the hell that meant, but when he saw Beckett nod out of the corner of his eye, he let it slide. He got the gist of it; they had no idea who was writing the messages.

"Alright, fine. And the other thing? The thing about Dr. Moorfield?"

"Yeah, way back when there was a, uh, *incident*."

"Incident? What kind of incident?"

Drake leaned forward in his chair as he spoke.

"Hold up, I'm getting there. It was something that was serious enough to warrant a tribunal."

Tribunal? What the hell?

Drake bit his tongue and allowed Screech to continue uninterrupted.

"There are very few details about the incident online. Far as I can tell, these things usually stick within the walls of the university. It looks like if something happens with a professor, something serious, then the university puts together a tribunal of sorts, usually made up of university board members, and they play Judge Dredd and decided what happens."

Drake looked over at Beckett. He was nodding.

"Yeah, it usually only goes to tribunal if it's really serious," Beckett said. "Otherwise, they just get an arbitrator to come in to sort things out."

"And in this case…?"

Screech shrugged.

"No way to tell. But like Beckett said, it must have been serious to warrant a tribunal."

Drake felt his frustration begin to mount. Evidently, he had mistaken Screech's sugar high for excitement.

"Well let's check with Chase then; if it's serious enough for Arthur's round table, maybe it was serious enough to get the police involved."

Beckett clucked his tongue.

"Yeah, I doubt that. After all, the university's reputation is critical to their success. I doubt it went to the police."

Drake threw up his hands.

"Fuck. This is ridiculous. Well then, gimme some goddamn examples of what kind of shit leads to these damn tribunals."

Drake felt like he was in a time warp, transported back to Dr. Kruk's office speaking in thinly veiled hypotheticals again.

"Plagiarism, relationships with a student, drug abuse, shit like that," Beckett said. "Theft, maybe. Sexual assault."

Drake chewed his lip as he thought about this. It might not be much, but he got the feeling that they were on the right track. Now it was just a matter of filtering through the debris.

He turned to Beckett.

"Looks like we should pay this doctor a visit. What do you think?"

Beckett's expression soured.

"Been there, done that. She's, uh, she's a real treat."

"A treat? How so?"

"Well, you know how it feels going bareback with a woman with vaginal atrophy?"

Drake blinked long and slow.

"What? What the hell are you talking about?"

Beckett shook his head.

"Nothing—never mind. She's just an old crust bag, is all. I doubt we can pry anything out of her."

Drake's thoughts once again turned inward. If Dr. Moorfield wouldn't talk, maybe they could pry information from members of the tribunal.

"Hey Screech, do you know who was part of the tribunal?"

"Dr. Moorfield and whoever—" Screech began, but Drake stopped him by waving a hand.

"No, I mean, who were the members of the board that served on the tribunal, to decide her fate or whatever the hell they did."

Screech shrugged.

"I don't know for sure, but like Beckett said, they are mostly made up of board members. That's public information, so I should be able to get you a list from back then."

"Good," Drake said, before turning to Beckett. "You ready?"

"For what?"

"To talk to the doctor. Have a nice little chat. What do you say?"

Beckett made a disgusted face.

"I say that—"

His phone rang, and he held up a finger while he looked at the screen.

"It's Chase," he said. "I gotta take this."

Chapter 52

"Where are we going?" Suzan asked in a small voice. She wiped the tears from her eyes, trying to focus on the road before her.

The point of the blade dug deeper into the side of her neck and she felt warm blood trace a line down to the collar of her shirt.

"Stop talking. Just do as I say."

Suzan whimpered and wiped more tears from her eyes. When her father had been alive, he had kept her isolated from the horrible crimes that he had investigated, the brutal murders that kept him up at night. Now, however, she wished that he had told her more, given her something that she might be able to use. The only thing she could remember—be it from him or from TV, she couldn't recall—was that staying quiet was a recipe for ending up dead. She had to keep the shadowy figure in the back seat talking. She had to remind him that she was a human being. That she had a right to live.

"What do you want from me?" she asked. The knife dug in a little deeper, and she felt a jolt of pain shoot down her arm. She ground her teeth and continued, undeterred. "Please, I have money. I can pay you. You can take the car if you want."

The blade moved again and Suzan inhaled, steeling herself against what she thought would be a slash that would open her throat.

But it never came.

Instead, the blade pulled away from her skin.

"You think I want money? Is that what you think this is about? *Money?*"

Suzan wasn't sure how she should answer this, but knew that she had to keep him talking.

"Everything is about money," she offered.

The man scoffed.

"C'mon, Suzan. You're smarter than that. If I was after money, then why would I kill drifters? A junkie in Central Park?"

"Eddie had money; he was a doctor."

The comment seemed to surprise the man in the backseat and he hesitated before answering. Suzan seized this opportunity to glance up at the rearview mirror, to get a good look at him in case she ever did manage to escape.

The man was wearing a makeshift ski-mask, the only openings being two ragged holes for his eyes. Even his mouth was covered, which explained why his speech was muffled. She squinted, trying to make out his eyes, but it was too dark in the car and she couldn't even manage to make out their color.

There was, however, something that she did notice: the faint smell of charcoal, maybe, or of a campfire, that hadn't been there before.

The smudges on the bodies.

And then it struck her, and she cursed herself for not putting it together before. The gray marks on the bodies that reminded her of Ash Wednesday were indeed ashes, and the man in the backseat was the *Arsonist*.

So stupid... if I had only thought about that before, I never would have agreed to meet him.

"Eddie was putting his nose where it shouldn't belong," the man said at last. "Budding in when he should have just minded his own damn business." The knife pressed against her neck again, and Suzan inhaled sharply. "Which is something you should have done, Suzan. I mean, c'mon... posting about forensic pathology? Acting coy? Did you really think I was gonna fall for that? The only thing you accomplished was letting me know that someone out there is looking for me. And you ending up here, of course."

Suzan swallowed hard.

"It doesn't matter. There are only two left, Suzan. Two left and then this will all be over."

"Two what?" Suzan whispered, even though she already knew that answer.

The man in the backseat chuckled.

"Two accidents, of course. Just two more than I will have finally completed the course. You're going to be number seven, Suzan, and I have a special treat in store for you and number eight."

He laughed again, and this time the sound grated on Suzan's ears. It wasn't a normal laugh, an involuntary expression of pleasure, but something darker. It was the laugh of a psychopath.

Any hope that Suzan had that her captor would suddenly grow a conscience, as fleeting as it might have been, was now completely and utterly crushed.

This man was cool, calm, and calculated. He had a plan, and Suzan was beginning to lose hope that anybody would be able to stop him, least of all herself.

Chapter 53

CHASE DUG A TOE into the gravel road as she spoke into her phone.

"Beckett, there's been—wait, who's there with you? Suzan?"

"Nuh-uh. I'm here with Drake and Screech. What's up?"

Chase sighed.

"There's been another murder, Beckett. Electrocution; tow truck driver on the outskirts of the city, looks like it happened a few hours ago."

Her eyes drifted to the body of Toby Teagar, a forty-four-year-old tow truck driver, a father of seven.

"Shit," Chase muttered, shaking her head. She was used to death, and even to murder, as much as one could become comfortable with the heinous act, but this was different. It was different because she knew how the next victim was going to die, and it was all taking a toll on her.

"Dammit," Beckett said. "What happened?"

"I don't know—this one is messed up. It looks like the tow truck driver was charging a battery by the side of the road when something went wrong; the scene is staged to make it look like he accidentally clipped one of the leads to his neck. Burnt right through his thin coat and shirt. No sign of any other car. This one… it's not as neat as the others. I mean, why would the tow truck driver be charging a battery at the side of the road? And how the hell did he manage to electrocute himself? I don't know if our killer is getting sloppy, or if he's just desperate to get to the end of his fucked up game. Either way, I can't see it taking more than another day or so before he kills again."

Hearing the words as they came out of her mouth made her feel sick to her stomach.

"Beckett? You still there?"

"Yeah. I'm gonna put you on speaker phone, hold on a sec."

Chase waited.

"Drake here; Drake and Screech."

Drake's voice was comforting.

"We have another one, Drake. Electrocution."

"I heard. The killer's cooling off period is getting shorter. Shit, I wouldn't be surprised if he already has his next victim picked out."

"Wait," Beckett interrupted. "Did you say that the guy shocked himself with a car battery?"

Chase glanced over at Toby's body again. He was lying at his back, his vacant eyes aimed upward.

"Yep, it's certainly made to look that way."

Beckett cleared his throat.

"Yeah, sorry, but it's just not possible."

"What do you mean?"

"It's a myth. You can't even get a shock from a car battery, let alone electrocute yourself. It's only twelve volts. The source of the electricity must have been something else."

Chase looked around again. They were on a dirt road, with nothing but... what had Detective Yasiv said? Weeds and allergies. Yeah, that was a fairly apt description.

"I don't know what to tell you, Becket, but that's how it's been staged. Anyways, it doesn't really matter how he died, only that it looks exactly like the photo from the exam."

There was only silence from the other end of the line.

He's getting sloppy and no longer cares if his crime scenes are ruled homicides instead of suicides or accidents. Either he's not worried about getting caught, or he's moving so quickly that he doesn't think we can catch him in time.

Chase hoped it was the former, but she had a sneaking suspicion that the latter was the case.

"Throat slit—with hesitation marks."

"Excuse me?" Chase said, coming out of her own head.

"The next one," Beckett replied. "Is a woman with her throat slit with hesitation marks. Hey Chase, can you do me a favor?"

Chase squatted by the body of the tow truck driver, indicating the other uniforms to take a step back.

"Yeah, go ahead."

"Check for any marks on the vic's skin; kinda like a small smudge of ashes."

Chase leaned close to the singe mark on the man's shoulder, peering through the hole in his shirt and jacket.

"You mean around the wound? His skin is all black and charred."

"No, no, not around the wound. Somewhere else. Somewhere that isn't related to the injury."

Chase's eyes narrowed and she searched the body. There was nothing on his hands, which had started to stiffen, or on his face, either.

"Naw, I don't see—hold on a sec."

She leaned over the man's neck, looking at the side opposite the wound. There, just below her ear, she saw what looked exactly like what Beckett had described: a smudge of soot or ash.

"Yeah, there's something here—on his neck. What is it? What's this about?" Chase asked as she stood.

"It's on all the bodies. I'm not sure what it is; I've got my tech guy on it, but he hasn't come back yet. No fingerprints, unfortunately, but he's going to tell me what it is and hopefully where it came from."

"A calling card?" she asked.

Drake answered her.

"Certainly looks that way. We found something else, too. Something about a website where people send messages? Like a—hold on a sec," when he spoke next, he was barely audible. "A what? Bulletin Board?" his voice became clear again, "Chase, Screech wants to talk to you."

"Alright, go ahead."

"It wasn't a website, but a bulletin board. I think that Eddie was posting on there, communicating with someone with the handle Arsonist514. Things went silent about a month ago, but then just the other day someone started posting in the thread again. A, uh, hold on… someone who goes by SC123. Anyways, seems like it might be related, given the ash or soot or whatever."

SC123?

"I already have Dunbar trying to find anything about med students, I'll get him on the website thing as soon as we wrap up here."

"Bulletin board," Screech corrected.

"Right. Can you pass the phone to Beckett for a sec?"

Chase heard the phone being passed around.

"Yeah, Beckett here. What's up?"

"Am I off speaker?"

"Yep."

"Do you know if Suze—" and then it hit her.

SC123. Suzan Cuthbert 123.

"Fuck," she gasped.

"What? What is it?"

"SC123? You think that it could be Suzan Cuthbert—SC? Have you spoken to her in a while?"

There was a short pause, during which she heard Beckett's breathing pick up as if he was walking briskly.

"No," he said quietly. "I haven't seen her since yesterday when we were together. Told her to get back to class."

Chase chewed her lip.

"Fuck, I hope to god that she listened. Go check on her, would you?"

"Yeah, I'll give her a ring. I'm sure she's fine. Tough as nails, that one. She was the one who found the soot, by the way. Listen, do you need me to come out there to clear the body?"

Chase shook her head.

"No, there's a junior ME already on scene. He'll bring the body back to you. I'll talk to Rhodes again, see if I can get him to open an investigation. This is the only death that I can see him having a hard time chalking it up to an accident, staged as it is, especially given what you told me about the battery. I don't know if I can get the stubborn bastard to bend, but we need more manpower on this, Beckett. He's going to kill again. And soon."

Chapter 54

Drake left Triple D in a fog of confusion.

Another victim, so soon after the last. And only two more to go.

He and Beckett had planned to go together to speak to Dr. Tracey Moorfield, but at the last minute, his friend had pulled the chute, telling him that he had to follow up on something at the morgue.

Drake had felt a twang of jealousy when Chase had asked to speak to Beckett privately, but he thought it was more than simple jealousy. They were keeping something from him.

Something that they didn't want him to know.

Drake shook his head, trying to clear his thoughts.

Stay focused. There will be time to find out what their big secret is later.

He made his way across the city to the university, taking the route suggested by Beckett. He parked and then strode through the cool evening toward the faculty club, where Beckett had assured him that Dr. Tracey Moorfield would be.

Despite his friend's assertions that he wasn't going to get anything out of her, it was still worth a shot. Officer Dunbar and Screech had their computers, but there was still a role for good old fashioned police work.

He hoped.

The door emblazoned with the gold plaque bearing Dr. Tracey Moorfield's name was ajar, and Drake knocked heavily so that it opened wider with every rap.

"Dr. Moorfield?"

He heard someone clear their throat.

"Yes? Who is it?"

Drake put a hand on the door and pushed it open, leaning into the opening. A well-dressed woman with thin lips drawn into a frown, not entirely unlike Mrs. Armatridge and her cronies, sat in a large wooden chair, papers spread out before her atop a massive desk.

"Dr. Moorfield?" he said again, putting on his most charming smile.

"That's what it says on the plaque, doesn't it? Unless the university decided to change that, too."

The smile slid off Drake's face.

What had Beckett said? She's like going bareback with a woman with vaginal something or other?

He shuddered at the thought of vaginal *anything* with this woman.

"What do you want?"

Drake stepped into the room.

"Did I say you can enter?"

Taken aback by this, Drake froze mid-step.

Dr. Moorfield sighed heavily.

"Well, you're already in now. I'll ask you once more, what do you want?"

Drake put his foot down and decided to forgo any small talk. He doubted if academic offices had emergency buttons beneath their desks like they did at the bank, but if they did, he suspected he only had a few seconds before Dr. Moorfield's arthritic digits pushed it.

"I'm here to ask you a few questions. About six murders."

One of the woman's eyebrows raised, and she put her pencil down on the desk.

"Are you a police officer?"

"No, not exactly."

Dr. Moorfield frowned.

"Not exactly? You're either a police officer, or you aren't. There is no in between. Which one is it?"

"I'm not," Drake said flatly.

"So why is a civilian coming to my office to ask questions about murder?"

Drake grimaced and he considered that Beckett might have understated the crust on the doctor.

"Well, I was a police officer once—a detective, but—"

Dr. Moorfield held up a hand, stopping him mid-sentence.

"I'm not interested in your life story. What do you want?"

Drake's blood pressure started to increase.

"These murders... the killer is copying your pathology notes. I believe that my friend, Dr. Campbell visited you earlier?"

Dr. Moorfield scowled.

"They let anyone become doctors these days. In my time, you had to be intelligent to be a doctor. Now, it seems all you need is hair dye and tattoos."

Drake felt like they were having two separate conversations, and he tried to get them back on track.

"Right, well I think that the killer might have been a former student of yours. Is there anyone that you can think of that might have been... I don't know, different? Someone with a vendetta, maybe?"

The woman's eyes went dark and a brief silence fell over the office.

"Get out," Dr. Moorfield said. "Get out of my office."

Drake held his hands up.

"Dr. Moor—"

"*Get out!*" she suddenly shrieked. "I don't know who you are, or why you are coming up with nonsense about murders only to bring up something that happened years ago, but I'm not falling for this."

"Dr. Moorfield, I—"

"Get out! Get out! Get the hell out of here!"

For such a small woman, such a wire rack of a human being, Dr. Tracey Moorfield certainly had a set of lungs on her.

Ears ringing, Drake stood in the office for a moment, trying to wrap his head around what had precipitated this. Then, watching as the elderly woman's chest heaved up and down, fearing that she was going to have a heart attack or a stroke, he spun on his heels and left the office.

"What the hell was that?" he grumbled on the way back to his car.

Maybe good old fashioned police work was dead after all.

He took his cell phone from his pocket and dialed Screech's number.

"Screech, I'm going to need the names of the people on the tribunal board. Beckett was right, I'm—"

But then he spotted something in the parking lot that drew his attention and he stopped speaking.

"What the hell?"

He squinted into the evening at a sleek black motorbike parked not twenty spots from his own.

Beckett's bike.

Only Beckett had said that he had urgent business at the morgue, not at the university.

Oh, there was a secret all right. And Drake hated being out of the loop.

Chapter 55

"COME ON, SUZE, PICK up your damn phone," Beckett grumbled. At first, he thought that Chase was just being paranoid, that there was no way that *SC123* was Suzan, trying to get in touch with the internet persona that might very well be their killer. But now, after trying her at home, and having to make up some story about Suzan missing class to appease her mother's anxiety, and calling her on her cell phone a half-dozen times and her not picking up, he wasn't so sure.

And then there was her cryptic message—*Beckett, it's Suzan. I've found something online. Give me a shout when you get this.*

Beckett hurried into the NYU medical building as he listened to her phone ring. He walked briskly toward his office, hoping to find her inside.

She's asleep. She fell asleep at my desk. Or at the library. That's why I can't reach her.

But when Beckett made it to his office, his heart sank. The door was closed, and the lights were off.

That's okay, she just turned off the lights before taking a cat nap behind my desk, he thought, his mind trying desperately to convince him.

He tried the door, but it was locked.

She locked the door, too, just to be safe. After all, there's a murderer out there.

A robotic voice on the other end of the line told Beckett that the voicemail of the person he was calling was full. He swore, and then hung up the phone. Pulling his set of keys from his pocket, Beckett knew deep down, even before he threw the door wide and found the room empty, that Suzan Cuthbert wouldn't be inside.

"Damn," he muttered as he flicked on the lights. "Where the hell are you, Suze?"

Beckett slumped into his chair and swirled his mouse, waking his computer. Surprised that it was still on, he leaned forward and typed in his password.

A web browser was already open, and when Beckett saw the address at the top of the page, his heart skipped a beat.

"No, c'mon, this can't be happening."

Suzan had logged into the bulletin board, and there was a new message pending. His hand trembling, he scrolled over to the envelope icon and, after a deep breath, clicked on it.

"No," he moaned.

Beckett scrambled for his phone, quickly dialing Chase's number, his eyes locked on the private message from Arsonist514.

"Chase, we have a problem. A fucking huge problem," he said when she answered.

Beckett shook his head as he stared at the message, trying to will it away.

Okay Suzan, see you soon :).

Chapter 56

CHASE LEFT THE CRIME scene in the capable hands of Detective's Yasiv and Simmons and hurried back to the station. She wasn't looking forward to another meeting with Sergeant Rhodes, but at this point, she could see no way of avoiding it.

They had to catch the killer before he struck again.

If he hadn't already, that is.

Armed with photographs from the most recent crime scene, of poor Toby Teager, Chase raced across the city and pulled into 62nd precinct just as night descended on New York. She recognized the similarities between what was happening now and the Butterfly Killer case, but the most recent killer was a different beast entirely. Dr. Mark Kruk had murdered people who had tortured him in his youth, and while this in no way justified what he did, citizens of New York could rest easier knowing they weren't involved. Now, however, there was someone out there targeting random people, murdering them without hesitation, without remorse, all to fulfill some sick, twisted fantasy.

Yet that wasn't the worst part; the worst part was that there was a serial killer out on the streets of New York City—a serial killer who had already killed six—and nobody knew about it. She despised the media and their propensity for inciting panic with five-second sound bites, but there was something to be said for transparency. Without it, with all of NYC in the dark as a killer roamed their streets, Chase just felt dirty.

She kept her head low as she made her way to Sergeant Rhodes's office, making sure not to make eye contact with anyone that might serve to distract her.

With a deep breath, she knocked once on Rhodes's door and then opened it without waiting for an answer.

Rhodes looked up at her over top of round spectacles that were pulled low on his narrow nose as she stepped inside.

"Well come on in," he said with a frown.

"There's been another murder," Chase said.

As expected, her bluntness gained Rhodes's attention, and he lowered the newspaper he had been reading, which, Chase noted, was opened to pre-election polling results.

"Murders? Please tell me you're talking about the home invasion on 32nd Avenue. Please, *please* tell me that that's what you are referring to, Chase."

Chase shook her head and proceeded to place the photographs of Toby Teager on top of Rhodes's newspaper.

"You know I'm not here about that."

Rhodes made no effort to disguise his displeasure.

"Who the hell is this?" he said, indicating the photographs. "Is this the tow truck driver who managed to zap himself?"

Chase ignored the comment and took a step backward.

"Look at the photographs."

But Rhodes didn't look. He simply stared at her.

"Are you fucking serious with this shit, Detective Adams? We had this discussion already." He interlaced his fingers slowly. When he spoke next, his voice had acquired a low, husky tone that matched the expression on his face. "I'm going to give you one chance to pick these photographs off my desk and then get out of here. *One* chance."

Chase felt her face get hot.

"Just look at the pictures! There's no way that this man, who spent twenty-two years as a tow truck driver somehow, oh, I dunno, managed to slip and accidentally clip the jumper cables to his neck and shoulder. The ME even says that it's impossible to electrocute yourself from a car battery! Not only that, but we found a calling card on all of the bodies—a smudge of dirt. There's a murderer out there, Rhodes, someone who has killed six people already, someone who won't stop until he finishes the course... until eight people are dead. And even then, I don't know if he'll be done."

Chase was breathing heavily when she finished, but it felt good to finally get it off her chest. She even thought that Rhodes, despite what he had said, might also be receptive to her words, given the way he just sat there, stone-faced.

"Maybe our tow truck driver was just sick and tired of living? Hmm? You ever think of that? Maybe he just offed himself like all the others."

Chase opened her mouth to say something, but Rhodes continued before she could make a sound.

"A *smudge?* A fucking smudge? Really? You found a smudge on the body of a man who's *been electrocuted?* Do you realize how stupid that sounds? And the other bodies? Do you have photographs of the other victims of their *smudges?*"

Chase shook her head.

"I—I—" *gave them to you already*, she intended to say before Rhodes once again cut her off.

"I told you already; I won't listen to this crap. Not now, not ever. Get out of my office and go home, Chase."

Chase looked up at the Sergeant, surprised at how calm he appeared. Somehow, this demeanor was even worse than him yelling and screaming at her, his face turning the ruby-red shade of an overripe tomato.

"Go home. Go home and stay home. A week, maybe more. If I see you around here before I call you, you're done."

Chase simply gawked.

"Wh-wh-what?"

Sergeant Rhodes curled his lips.

"Pick up your photographs and get the hell out of here," he hissed.

"But—"

Rhodes suddenly swept his hand across his desk, sending the images of Toby Teager flying across the floor.

"Pick up the damn photographs and get out!" Rhodes shouted. "*Get the hell out!*"

Rhodes's voice was so loud that it snapped Chase out of her stupor and she scrambled to scoop up the photographs.

She looked up one final time at Rhodes's now red face and debated getting the final word in.

You're going to regret this, Rhodes. I promise, you're going to regret this.

Deciding that saying another word would end her career, Chase bit her tongue and left the office, more frustrated than she had been when she had arrived.

Sure, she would leave for a week, or however long Rhodes suspended her, but there was one thing she had to do first.

Walking briskly, again with her head low, she made her way to the stairwell and opened the door to the subbasement.

At the end of the long, dark hallway, was the door to *Records*. Chase was surprised to see Dunbar standing in the doorway staring at her as she approached.

Word travels fast in this precinct, she thought with a grimace.

"Dunbar, things have escalated. There's someone I think you should meet."

Chapter 57

THE GAG WAS FILTHY, and every time her tongue brushed up against the coarse material, Suzan felt vomit rise in her throat. Tears streaked her cheeks, making muddy tracks through the soot that covered her face.

The man in the mask had directed her to a condemned building nestled near the end of a quiet cul-de-sac. During the drive, Suzan had tried to keep track of the directions, to map the direction to the house, but this had proven difficult, what with the tears that filled her eyes, and the fear that coursed through her veins.

She knew that they weren't far from the university campus, ten miles, fifteen max, but it wasn't a location she recognized.

"Stop here," the man in the mask grumbled. He then instructed her to get out of the car.

Suzan stepped into the night and for one, fleeting moment, thought that she could run. But then she felt the knife tip press into her spine, and the fantasy of escaping vanished.

"Move," the man instructed, and Suzan obeyed.

He led them down the side of the house, staying low, warning her that if she shouted, he would drive the knife through her spine. The windows were all boarded up, but the man easily peeled a piece of plywood back—Suzan got the impression by the way it came free easily that this wasn't his first time removing it—and then she was forced inside.

Most of the walls on the ground level had been removed, torn down to the studs. Where walls remained, they were streaked with floor to ceiling scorch marks. Even though it was obvious that the fire that had ripped the two-story colonial had happened many years prior, the smell of burnt wood was still strong in the stale air.

"Upstairs," the man ordered.

Suzan felt her legs go weak and threaten to buckle.

"Please," she tried to say, but the gag rendered the word unintelligible.

"Now!"

Sobbing, Suzan took the steps slowly, one foot in front of the other, worried that at any moment she would lose control of her limbs and fall backward, impaling herself on the eight-inch blade in the process.

But somehow, with strength she hadn't known she possessed, Suzan made it all the way to the top.

The floor of the second floor was warped, with large sections removed, revealing singed floorboards beneath. The walls, however, had fared better on this level and remained mostly intact.

The man led her to a room without a door, but with four complete walls. He forced her to a seated position, and before she knew it, her hands were bound behind her back with lengths of worn rope that looked too much like the section that had been wrapped around Eddie's neck to be a coincidence.

Suzan wept as the man started to set up a tripod and camera across from her. He worked quickly, but without giving the impression that he was rushed. He was clearly not worried about anyone interrupting them.

"Please," she tried to say again, but once again the word was muffled by the filthy gag.

The man didn't even acknowledge her. After locking the camera on top of the tripod, he got behind it and then proceeded to focus the lens on her.

Suzan shook her head, causing her hair, damp with sweat, to fall in front of her face. It was a petty maneuver, but the only thing that she could control.

He can kill me, but I won't give him the satisfaction of seeing my face when he does.

She was disappointed when the man didn't seem bothered by her petulance.

Apparently satisfied, the masked man clapped his hands together and Suzan's body jolted as if shocked by electricity. She was sobbing uncontrollably now, her entire body quaking.

The man strode over to her and crouched down low, tilting his head to one side as he observed at her. At first, Suzan refused to look, but when it became apparent that he wasn't about to leave without making eye contact, she flipped her hair back and stared.

The man had pale blue eyes that seemed out of place buried in the black leather mask. Paradoxically, they seemed like caring eyes. Soft, placating.

"You made a mistake, Suzan. This didn't have to be you. You just had to stay out of it, mind your business."

Suzan wanted to say something, wanted to yell in his face that it still didn't have to be her, but she didn't say anything.

Even without a gag, terror so gripped her that she would have struggled to form a single word.

The man in the mask reached behind him, and Suzan cowered, thinking that he was going to pull out his knife and cut her throat right there on the burnt hardwood, before snapping his macabre photographs.

She wondered, strangely, if the photos would get back to her mother, and how she would cope after losing both her husband and daughter to different serial killers.

Jasmine Cuthbert was a strong woman, she had to be, but everyone had their breaking point.

Suzan couldn't imagine that her mother would come out of this with her sanity intact.

But it wasn't a knife that the man pulled out, but another section of rope. He wrapped it around her ankles, pulling her legs together tightly as he tied it.

After he was done, he patted her on the knee.

"There, now sit tight. And don't worry, you won't be alone for long. Soon, you're going to have company."

The masked man stood and before she could even blink, he was gone from the room. Less than thirty seconds later, she heard the sound of a car—*her* car—starting up. And then that too faded away.

Suzan allowed herself one more sob, one more deep breath, and then she started to look for a way to escape.

Chapter 58

"OFFICER ROBERT DUNBAR, MEET Screech," Chase said as she stepped into Triple D. Drake's eyes lifted from behind his desk.

What the hell?

The introduction surprised Screech as well, and he made a face before shaking Dunbar's hand.

"Hi," Screech said hesitantly.

"Dunbar is going to help with the search—he has access to certain databases that you can't get into," Chase said flatly.

Officer Dunbar nodded and then turned to Screech.

"Chase says you're pretty good with computers."

Screech took the compliment in stride.

"Well, Chase is a smart woman. Here, let me show you what I got," he said, guiding Officer Dunbar over to his computer in the reception area.

"See if you can find out anything at all about Dr. Moorfield and who this damn student or faculty member she went to the tribunal with all those years ago."

"Got it," Dunbar said.

Beckett entered Triple D next, a deep frown on his face. His blond hair, usually spiked, lay flat against his head. He looked tired and oddly *old*.

As Drake watched, Chase and Beckett exchanged a look and then a nod before coming toward him together.

"What's going on with you two?" Drake asked, the words coming out with more venom than he had expected. "Are you guys going to clue me in on your little secret, or what?"

Chase bowed her head as she entered his office. Beckett followed closely, closing the door after they were all inside.

"What the fuck's going on, guys?"

It was Beckett who answered.

"It's my fault," he began quietly. "I brought her onboard."

Drake's eyes narrowed.

Her?

"Who? What are you talking about?"

Beckett shook his head and appeared to be speaking to himself now.

"I just thought… shit, she was my TA, and I thought that she… she just wanted to help."

Drake felt his frustration reach a peak and he jumped out of his chair. He started toward Beckett, but Chase stepped between them.

"It's Suzan, Drake. He's got Suzan."

Drake's entire world collapsed.

"Suzan?" he heard himself say, but had no idea that he was actually articulating the words. "Suzan Cuthbert?"

Drake felt as if he were falling forward, but Chase wrapped her arms around him, preventing him from going down. And then Beckett was there, too, guiding him back to his chair.

The rain was coming down heavily, soaking both him and Clay as they stood outside Peter Kellington's house.

"Should I announce our presence?" Clay asked as he peered through the gap between the door and the frame.

"Should I?"

Then Clay started to turn, and as he did his features became softer, the beard fading, the dark hair on his head growing longer and becoming straighter.

"Should I, Drake?" Suzan Cuthbert asked, the rain streaking her cheeks like tears. "Drake? What should I do?"

"Fuck, Drake. Snap out of it. We need you."

Drake blinked hard, then shook the fog from his mind. Without thinking, his hand shot out and he grabbed Beckett by the throat. And then he started to squeeze.

"You brought Suzan into this?" he hissed.

"Drake, let him go!" Chase shouted.

Drake ignored her.

"You fucking brought her into this?"

Beckett was grabbing at the hand wrapped around his throat, but he was no match for Drake and his grip.

A croak came out of Beckett's mouth, and his eyes started to bulge.

"Why, Beckett? Why did you bring her into this?"

But Beckett couldn't answer—he was being strangled.

A hand suddenly stung Drake's face. It wasn't a hard slap, but it startled him enough that his grip on Beckett's throat slipped.

When he saw the look on Chase's face, he let go completely.

Beckett coughed and spat, and then doubled over, hands on his knees, trying to catch his breath.

"Fuck, I'm sorry," Drake grumbled. "Shit. *Shit!*"

Beckett still doubled over, held up a hand.

"It's alright," he said between coughs. "I'm fine."

Drake looked over at Chase and saw something in her eyes that he had never seen before.

Fear.

She had been scared when Dr. Mark Kruk had kidnapped her and tied her up, put a gun to her head.

But now she was scared of *him*. Of her ex-partner.

"I'm sorry," he repeated.

"It's over now," Chase replied, and then she proceeded to tell him about Suzan's involvement, starting with her helping with Beckett and his forensic pathology exam to the messages that Beckett had read on the bulletin board less than an hour ago.

"And no one has seen her since?" Drake asked.

Chase shook her head.

"No. I had two friends in blue go by her house and ask around campus. Nothing. No trace of her. Her car is gone, but no one saw anything."

"Fuck," Drake said under his breath.

"Can Dunbar or Screech trace her cell phone? Her car?"

Again, Chase shook her head.

"It'll take too long—she just vanished, Drake."

Drake's demeanor, after the outbreak with Beckett, had suddenly become calm, calculated. While he had previously been driven to stop a killer who had murdered six people, now his approach was more singular.

To get Suzan Cuthbert back.

To get her back alive.

"Does Jasmine Cuthbert know?"

Beckett answered this time, his voice hoarse.

"No, she has no idea."

Drake jumped to his feet, and a pang of guilt struck him when both Chase and Beckett recoiled slightly.

"Find out who the fuck this guy is," he snapped as he strode toward the door.

"Where are you going? What are you going to do?" Chase hollered after him.

"I'm going to speak to Dr. Moorfield again. This time she's going to tell me what the fuck happened at the tribunal—she's going to tell me, or wish she had."

Chase step forward.

"I'm coming with you."

Drake frowned.

"No way. You stay here, help Dunbar and Screech. If they find anything, I need you here to act quickly."

Drake hurried toward the door, aware that his reality had acquired a dreamlike state that reminded him of his nightmares of the evening Clay Cuthbert had been murdered.

This can't be happening.

His hand had just fallen on the doorknob when Beckett grasped his arm. He half expected the man to strike him, but when he saw the look of determination in his eyes, he knew that this wasn't the case.

Beckett couldn't believe that this was happening either, and now he shared Drake's solitary goal.

"I'm coming with you," he said. Drake stared at his friend for a moment, then nodded.

Chase couldn't come with him, because she was still an NYPD Detective. And he feared that he might have to resort to 'good ol' fashioned police work again in order to extract information from Dr. Moorfield. Chase couldn't be there for that; she couldn't be a witness to it.

Beckett, on the other hand…

"Fine," he snapped.

On the way past the reception area, Screech suddenly leaped to his feet, a piece of paper in hand.

"Drake, take this."

"What is it?" he asked without breaking stride.

"The list of board members when Moorfield went to the tribunal."

Drake snatched the paper and continued toward the door.

"Find her, Screech. Please, for the love of god, find Suzan Cuthbert."

Chapter 59

UNDER NORMAL CIRCUMSTANCES, THE drive from Triple D to the faculty club would have taken close to thirty minutes. But with Drake driving like a maniac, it took less than half that time.

They rode in silence. Twice Drake saw Beckett open his mouth to say something, before deciding better of it, which was fine by him. He had lashed out, warranted or not, and then apologized. It wasn't the first time that he and Beckett hadn't seen eye-to-eye, and it certainly wouldn't be the last.

There was no time to be bogged down by sore throats and hurt feelings.

Drake double-parked directly in front of the doors to the faculty club and leaped from his Crown Vic while it was still running.

"Dr. Moorfield was too concerned with getting called out for what happened in the past to give me anything before," he said as Beckett hurried to keep up with him. "She didn't believe that I was telling the truth about the murders, thought I was just trying to pry information from her. Maybe now, though, now that the killer has Suzan, she'll be more open. And if not, there are ways of making people talk. Even those as stubborn as Dr. Moorfield."

Drake wasn't sure if he was speaking to Beckett or just thinking out loud, but felt reassured when his friend chimed in.

"Yeah, maybe. I mean, Suzan was a medical student after all. I just... shit, the woman is just so damn *obstinate*."

Drake nodded as Beckett scanned his keycard at the front door, gaining them access to the faculty club.

"And if we can't get anything from her, I've got eight other names to look up," he said, pulling the piece of paper that Screech had given him from his pocket and waving it in the air. "We're going to find her, Beckett. We're going to find her, and she's going to be alive when we do."

And yet, despite his reassuring words, images of Suzan filled his mind, flashing so rapidly that before he could completely grasp what he was seeing, the imaginary menagerie was onto the next. First, she was bent over her own neck, then in the bathtub, her eyes milky, her wrists slit. Next, she was hanging from the ceiling, shirtless, her tongue thick, followed by an image of her lying on her back, the top of her head rendered organic confetti. The penultimate image was of Suzan with burn marks on her shoulder and neck, her long brown hair frizzled, standing on end.

And then, finally, she was lying on the sidewalk, her throat opened in a crimson grin.

Drake shuddered.

"Let's go!" he shouted suddenly, breaking into a jog. "Let's go!"

As expected, the door to Dr. Moorfield's office was open, just as he had left it not more than a few hours ago. But when Drake burst through, Beckett in tow, he was surprised to find it empty.

"Shit," he swore, eyes whipping around. They fell on Beckett. "Where is she? Do you have her number?"

Beckett looked as if he was on the verge of breaking into tears.

"I don't know... I don't have her number."

Furious, Drake moved around to the other side of the desk, scanning the messy top for any hints or clues as to where she might have headed.

"Fuck!" he yelled. With one arm, he swiped the contents off the desk in a fit of anger. As the medical journals, loose papers, and a stack of pens fell to the floor with a clatter, his eyes immediately focused on the burnished wood beneath.

"Beckett," he said, his eyes locking in on the desktop. Beckett, who was busy looking at his phone, presumably searching for Dr. Moorfield's contact info, glanced up.

"What? What is it?"

Drake gestured to the desk.

"Look!" he exclaimed, eyes wide. "*Look!*"

Beckett hurried to his side. When he saw the words on the wood, drawn using the same soot or ash as the marks on the murder victims, Drake heard him suck in a tight breath.

"We have to go," Drake said. "We have to hurry. He's going to finish this—he's going to kill Suzan and Dr. Moorfield tonight."

He pulled the paper Screech had given him from his pocket as he said this, unwilling to take his eyes from the words on the desk: *Two more.*

The killer had been here. Within the two hours since Drake had last been standing in this very office, the killer had been here.

So close—I was so close.

Someone shouted in the hallway, snapping Drake out of his state of panic.

He unfolded the paper and quickly scanned the names for any that looked familiar. If he didn't recognize any of them, he would start at the top, breaking down the doors of each until he found the information he needed, the information that would lead them to the killer.

When his eyes fell on board member five of eight, he felt his breath catch in his throat. Swallowing hard, he folded the paper back and jammed it into his pocket.

Then he turned to Beckett.

"Let's go," he hissed. "Let's get out of here."

An overweight security guard with a utility belt so jammed full of tools that Batman would be jealous, suddenly appeared in the doorway of Dr. Moorfield's office.

"Halt!" he ordered, holding a can of pepper spray out in front of him in one chubby hand.

Drake didn't *'halt'*; he kept on moving forward.

"Get the fuck out of my way," he said, leveling his eyes at the man. The security guard faltered.

"Halt," he said again, but his voice lacked the bravado of his previous command.

Drake balled his fists, prepared to strike the man if he didn't move. But before he did, Beckett stepped forward and took control of the situation.

"NYPD," his friend said. "We're here investigating six murders and two kidnappings."

"Wh—what?" the fat man said, lowering the can of pepper spray a few inches.

"Dr. Moorfield's been kidnapped!" Drake shouted. "*Now out the fuck out of the way!*"

And then the man, driven by a combination of fear and confusion, slid to one side.

Drake didn't give the security guard a chance to reconsider. He pushed by him and then broke into a sprint, hoping, but not checking to see if Beckett was following.

Chapter 60

By manipulating her jaw, Suzan managed to slip the gag down to her chin. Finally able to breathe properly without the risk of vomiting, she took a moment to better observe her surroundings.

The floor on which she sat was charred and burnt, and most areas that were salvageable had since been removed by looters, revealing a sooty subfloor. By the doorway she noted a single plank of hardwood, jutting up at an odd angle. It appeared wedged beneath the doorway trim, which had probably made it too troublesome to remove by the person that had taken the rest of the floor.

Think, Suzan. Think.

She had seen enough movies in her time to know that the masked man wouldn't take long to return. And when he did…

Don't think about that. *Think about finding a way out.*

With her hands and feet bound, she had to shimmy on her ass to move across the floor. Even though the binds on her wrists were tight, she still managed to push down with her palms, lifting her lower body before sliding it over. It was a painful process and after just a few of these awkward movements, the muscles in her arms started to ache. And with every thrust, the ropes cut deeper into her wrists. But by using this technique, Suzan moved quickly to the jutting floor plank.

It was dark inside the house, but with the full moon outside, and some of the plywood on the upper floor not aligned properly, she noticed that in the process of trying to remove the flooring, a piece of metal framing had also been exposed near the intersection of the floor and the door trim.

Suzan, sweat now mixing with the tears and ash on her face, made her way next to the exposed metal, and then spun around. With a deep breath, she lowered the rope between her wrists onto the metal.

Her first strike caused the fire weakened metal to fold over and she cried out in frustration. But after lowering the rope a second time, she realized that it was now anchored in the burnt subfloor, and the sharp edge was even more exposed. Suzan worked cautiously at first, making sure that she didn't break the metal as she rubbed the rope against it. But as the seconds passed, she became more and more paranoid that the man in the mask was going to come sprinting up the stairs, and she started to work more furiously.

Every other stroke missed the mark, and she could feel blood running down into her palms as the metal sliced into her skin.

"Come on, come one," she whispered as she worked.

And then, after it felt as if the entire night had passed, Suzan felt the rope give a little. With a tremendous grunt, she flexed and pulled her hands apart.

The frayed rope let go with a muted snap.

Yes! Her mind cried. Bringing her hands in front of her, she could see that they were covered in blood and noted several deep cuts in the skin on the pad of her palm.

Ignoring the damage, she immediately started to tug at the rope around her ankles. She had only just started to figure out the knot when she froze.

The sound of a car pulling into the driveway filled the hollow house.

"No," she moaned. Working frantically, she tried to pull the rope from her ankles, but in her desperation, she yanked the wrong loop and it tightened.

"Please..."

But tears obscured her vision and no matter what she tried, the binding only seemed to pull her ankles closer together.

She heard a car door open, followed by an abbreviated struggle.

The sound of the plywood window covering being removed reached her next, followed quickly by footsteps on the floor below.

Suzan closed her eyes.

It was too late; even if she managed to free her ankles, there was no way that she would be able to run downstairs and get past the masked man.

Shaking her head, she grabbed the torn rope and scuttled back to where he had left her, putting her now free arms behind her back.

She heard the man on the stairs, but was now keenly aware that there was someone else with him.

And judging by the high-pitched nature of the muffled screams, it was likely a woman.

A weapon... if only I had worked faster, I could have grabbed a weapon.

Just as a shadow filled the doorway, Suzan realized that her filthy gag was still off, and she pulled it up over her mouth.

A bound and gagged woman was shoved in her direction. She tripped over the raised piece of flooring and collapsed to the ground, her thin body sliding to a stop only inches from Suzan, who cowered away from her.

The masked man entered the room next.

"I told you I'd be back," he said with a chuckle. "And this time I brought company."

Chapter 61

DRAKE POUNDED ON THE glass door with both fists.

"Open up!" he yelled. "Open the fucking door!"

He looked over his shoulder at the Crown Vic and saw Beckett's shocked expression staring back from the passenger seat.

"Call them!" he yelled to the frightened man. "Call Chase!"

Beckett seemed frozen.

"Just fucking call them!"

A light flicked on from within the lobby of the condo, and he turned back. The security guard with the oak-colored mustache sauntered toward him, moving with the pace of a funeral procession.

"Open up!" Drake yelled again as he continued to bang on the glass. The security guard's eyes narrowed, and Drake saw him reach for something on his hip. At first, Drake thought he was reaching for the keys, but when he saw the man palm the butt of his gun, his heart sunk.

This was no university guard with a can of pepper spray.

"Please," Drake said, changing tactics. "Open the door. I need to talk to him."

The man moved closer to the door, but to Drake's dismay, he stopped a safe distance away. As he neared, he squinted, and then, finally, recognition crossed his face.

"Detective Drake? Is that you?"

"Yes, it's fucking me, now open the door?"

The security guard took a step backward.

"I'm afraid I can't do that. I've been—"

But a sound from behind him drew both of their attention. Drake peered over the man's shoulder, but could only make out the outline of a second man. They exchanged a few words in hushed voices, then the security guard turned back to Drake.

This time he had his keys in hand and was frantically trying to open the door. A second later, Drake heard the familiar click of the lock disengaging, and he shoved the glass door open, knocking the security guard backward.

"Wait! You need to—"

"Never mind that, Stewart. Come with me, Drake," the shadowy figure said, stepping into view.

Drake grimaced at the sight of the short, dark-skinned man with the wiry mustache.

"Raul, I need to speak to Ken. I need to speak to him *now*."

Raul nodded.

"*Jes*, he knows you are here. Please follow me."

Drake hurried after Raul, who had the elevator on call, the doors open and waiting for them. They stepped inside and Ken's manservant used a small key to set the elevator on its course to the penthouse.

The express ride to the forty-eighth floor seemed to take much longer than Drake remembered when he had been here a few months prior. Eventually, after what felt like an age listening to Raul's heavy mouth breathing, the elevator pinged and the doors started to open.

Drake pushed by Raul and stepped into Ken Smith's opulent penthouse apartment.

"Ken!" he shouted. "Ken, where are you?"

Ken Smith, dressed in a crisp gingham dress shirt and navy slacks stepped into view, a drink in hand, a wry smile on his lips. As usual, his gray hair was slicked back, not a single strange out of place.

"I'm here, Drake. No need to shout. Please, tell me what is so urgent that you—"

Drake finally managed a full breath.

"He's got Suzan. The bastard took Suzan."

Ken Smith ran a hand through his hair.

"Who? Who has Suzan? What the hell is going on, Drake?"

Drake grimaced, fighting back tears.

"A psychopath… he took her and Dr. Moorfield and he's going to kill them both."

There was a short pause, during which Ken's brow furrowed. It was only in this moment, with his forehead crinkled in concern that he actually started to look his age.

"Dr. Moorfield?"

"Yes. It's the man from the tribunal… whatever happened between them, he's seeking revenge now. Please, you have to tell me his name."

Ken simply stared at him.

"Please, you need to help me," Drake pleaded. "He's going to kill her! You have to—"

He stepped forward, intent on grabbing Ken's perfectly ironed shirt and shaking the man. But out of the corner of his eye, he caught sight of Raul, the short, stocky man, moving toward him with astonishing speed.

Drake let his hands fall to his sides.

"Please, Ken. I need—"

"Slow down," Ken said firmly. "Tell me what the hell is going on?"

"There's a man… a man with some sort of vendetta against Dr. Tracey Moorfield. He's been killing drifters, making it look like suicide. And now he has Suzan and Dr. Moorfield. You were… you were on the tribunal for something that Dr. Moorfield was involved in long ago. You need to help me, you have to tell me who was involved. You—"

Ken held up a hand, silencing him.

"I'm thinking, dammit. Give me a second."

Drake feared that seconds was all he had before Suzan's throat was slit.

"It was so long ago… I remember… I remember Dr. Moorfield was sleeping with a student, and… and…"

"Hurry, please."

Ken's brow furrowed again, and this time the creases extended to the corners of his eyes.

"Craig," he said softly, a far-off look in his eyes. "Dr. Moorfield was having an affair with Craig Sloan, a medical student. Things went badly, and…"

Drake didn't even acknowledge the rest of what Ken had to say. Instead, he yanked his phone from his pocket and sprinted back toward the elevator.

"Chase! Chase, the killer's name is Craig Sloan!" he shouted into the phone.

Drake looked up in time to see Ken standing in the hallway, his drink still clutched in his hand. And then, just as the doors silently closed, he thought he saw a smile form on the man's lips.

Chapter 62

THE BOUND WOMAN, WHO Suzan quickly realized was at least in her seventies, somehow managed to pull herself to a seated position. Despite the woman's advanced age, or perhaps because of it, the woman was oddly calm, whereas Suzan's body continually rocked with sobs.

And Suzan's fear only intensified when the masked man stepped in front of them and slid the blade from a sheath on his hip. He angled it so that the moonlight reflected off the steel.

"If you scream, I'll slice your carotid artery," he said as he stepped forward. When his filthy hand reached for Suzan, she closed her eyes tightly thinking that he was going to grab a fistful of hair and yank her head back, exposing the soft skin beneath her chin.

Please, just make it quick, she pleaded silently.

But instead of cold steel, Suzan felt the man's calloused fingers brush up against her cheek. In one smooth motion, he pulled Suzan's gag down and then proceeded to do the same to the woman beside her.

Whimpering, Suzan said, "Wh—what do you want from us?"

The man ignored her and brought the hand not holding the knife to the jagged bottom of the crudely made leather mask. His fingers tucked beneath it, and then he lifted it off his face.

He was handsome, with short brown hair, blue eyes, and the beginnings of a beard. His nose was slightly crooked, but wasn't bent enough to make him look sinister.

The woman tensed beside Suzan.

"You," she said softly, her eyes going wide.

"Ah, yes, *me,* Tracey—it's me. After fifteen years in prison, I'm back to finish what I started—to prove to you that I am a worthy student. When I'm done with you two, I will have completed the forensic pathology exam. I think this time I'll get a passing grade."

Suzan swallowed hard, her mind flicking to the final two images from Beckett's presentation.

Throat slit and...

Only then did she notice the red jerry cans of gasoline near the far wall.

She gasped.

The final test image was of a burnt corpse—he was going to burn one of them alive.

"You were a lousy student and a worse lover, Craig," Tracey spat.

Craig laughed.

"You think so? Well, I spent fifteen years working on my craft, my dear. Although the time for the latter has since past, perhaps I can impress you with the former."

He stepped forward with the knife outstretched and then crouched on his haunches.

"And you're going to help me."

Tracey scoffed.

"Help you? *Help you?* You really are delusional. You were delusional back then, and your time in prison hasn't changed that one bit."

Suzan's eyes whipped from Tracey to Craig to the knife and back again. She was having a difficult time keeping up with this manic conversation.

"Delusional? You ruined me, Tracey. I loved you, and you used that against me. Used it to ruin me. I lied for you... I lied for you at the goddamn tribunal to make sure you kept your job. And what did you do? You threw me under the bus, flunked me from your class. Tracey, I *loved* you."

"Loved me?" Tracey chuckled. "You may have loved me, Craig, but I never loved you. You were just a quick fuck, something to take my mind off my work. It's not my fault you latched on to me like an Oedipus leech. Everything that happened to you... everything from getting expelled, to lighting my house—*this* house—on fire is your doing. You need to grow up and live with the consequences of your decisions. You were a child back then, and you're still a child now."

Enraged, Craig leaned back and slapped the woman hard across the face. Suzan yelped, but Tracey didn't make so much as a whimper. Her head flung to one side, and as the echo of the slap died down, she slowly turned back to face their captor.

"Fuck you," she said, and then spat in Craig's face.

Suzan found herself shaking her head subconsciously and mumbling to herself.

What are you doing? Don't piss him off!

But Tracey's words stung Craig more than her saliva. He calmly wiped the wetness from his face and then, to Suzan's surprise, held the knife out to Tracey, handle first.

"You ruined my life, and now it's my turn to ruin yours."

"I won't do it," Tracey said, and for the first time since she had been shoved into the room, Suzan thought she detected fear in the woman's voice.

"Oh, you will, Tracey. Because here's the thing: you remember the test? You remember one through six?"

Tracey said nothing, and the man smiled broadly.

"Of course you do, after all, you made the damn thing. You see, the cops are stupid, but they aren't *that* dumb. I left a little hint, a little clue from this place at every scene. Every last one of them. And eventually, they'll put the pieces together. When they do, they'll know that you were behind it all. It's just too bad that you won't be around to witness it. I made a mistake with the folder—I didn't know that you had changed offices. But it doesn't matter; there's still enough evidence to link you to all of the murders. And based on your track record, I doubt the police will have to stretch too far to accept that you're the one responsible. I mean, doctors become a little strange when they're no longer relevant, don't they? Tucked away in an office, out of sight, working on some bullshit assignments. All alone in the dark, things can get lonely…"

The photographs… Craig had left them on Beckett's desk thinking that it was still Dr. Moorfield's office. And then Eddie found them… and… and…

Suzan's breath hitched.

Eddie was putting his nose where it shouldn't belong… budding in when he should have just minded his own damn business.

Tracey shook her head and then laughed out loud, a hideous, high-pitched cackle.

"You think they'll pin this on me? On *me*? You really are stupider than I thought. They are going to put it all on *you*, Craig. How can you not see that? After all, you spent fifteen years in prison for burning this place down. And you came to my defense at the tribunal? Really? You simple idiot, they couldn't fire me even if they wanted to, I had—and still have—tenure. But me… I testified at your trial, told the defense that I was usually out on Tuesday nights, and that this is something that you would have known."

The man seemed to consider this for a moment, his smile fading.

"It's not true," he said softly.

Tracey laughed again.

"Oh, it's true. Think about it. If the judge thought you knew I was in the house when you set it on fire, you would still be in prison for attempted murder, Craig."

The kind expression in the man's pale blue eyes returned, but this only lasted for a moment. He shook his head.

"It doesn't matter. It's almost over now, the test is almost through. And in my unbiased opinion, I think I'm about to pass with flying colors."

He held out the knife again, blade first this time.

"Take the knife, Tracey. Take the knife and slit her throat or I swear to god that I'll cut you slow. You may think you are tough, but I learned more than just pathology during my time in prison. I will make you wish you were dead ten times over."

With one deft slice, Craig released Tracey from the ropes that bound her wrists.

"Take it," he repeated, his eyes blazing.

Suzan was crying again, and her sobs only increased when Tracey reached out and retrieved the knife from Craig's hand.

Kill him! She wanted to scream, but couldn't manage the words. *Kill him!*

Tracey stared at the knife for a moment, before raising her eyes to look at Suzan.

Suzan saw the same gleam of hatred, of anger, of vile resentment in the woman's face that mirrored their captor's.

"No," she moaned. "Please don't do this."

In her mind, she clung to the notion that this was a trick, that the old doctor was going to pretend to cut her, then reach out and drive the knife into Craig's chest.

But those eyes… she's as batshit crazy as he is.

Instead of moving toward Craig, Tracey slid closer to Suzan. Through tear-streaked vision, she looked to Craig in desperation, praying that he would finally come to his senses and just let her go.

But when her eyes focused on the gun that had replaced the knife in his hand, the gun that was aimed directly at Tracey's narrow chest, she lost all hope.

"Do it, Tracey. Finish the test for me."

This can't be happening. She can't really be thinking about doing this.

"No, don't," Suzan pleaded. "Please."

But the steel in the woman's gray eyes made it clear that her mind was already made up. Before Suzan could get her arms out in front of her, forgetting up until this moment that she had freed them, Tracey lunged, driving the point of the knife into her throat.

Suzan gasped and fell backward with the force of the impact.

"Yes!" she heard Craig scream, but his voice now sounded far away. She felt blood start to flow down her neck, dampening her hair, and then Tracey was on top of her, her rail-thin body blocking Suzan's view of Craig.

The woman's thin, wrinkled fingers went to work, moving the knife back and forth.

Hesitation marks, Suzan thought absently. *Just like in the photograph.*

She closed her eyes, and Craig's laughter washed over her in waves.

"Yes! Yes! *Yes!*"

Then Suzan heard another sound — splashing liquid — followed by the caustic smell of gasoline.

As consciousness faded, a bright light flashed behind Suzan's closed lids, and she heard flames beginning to devour the previously scorched wood.

Chapter 63

"Drake? Slow down!" Chase said, pulling the phone away from her ear to avoid being deafened by Drake's shouts. "Craig Sloan? How do you know this is our guy?"

"I just met with Ken Smith—he was on the tribunal. Says that Dr. Moorfield was having a relationship with a student… Craig Sloan."

Chase nodded to herself, then turned to Dunbar.

"Dunbar, I need an address for Craig Sloane."

Dunbar whipped around, but Screech beat him to the keyboard. He hammered away on the keys for a few seconds.

"Craig Sloan, expelled from pathology residency," Screech said quickly, his eyes remaining locked on the screen. "Spent fifteen years in prison after being convicted of Class 1A arson for burning down his professor's house—Dr. Moorfield, I presume."

Chase moved to get a better look at the computer screen.

"Hold on, Drake," she said into her phone. A strangled gasp escaped the man's throat, followed by the sound of a car engine starting up. "Just hold the fuck on."

"Got out on parole eight months ago," Screech continued.

"Address, Screech. Give me a damn address."

"Working on it," Screech said as he continued to type. Another image flashed on screen, this time of a still smoldering colonial, a fire truck in the foreground. "Shit, I can't bring up anything recent."

"Lemme try," Dunbar offered, squeezing in beside Screech. Screech lifted his hands, relinquishing the keyboard to the officer. Chase watched intently as Dunbar pulled up the NYPD server, then navigated to the button in the upper right-hand corner of the screen marked PAROLE.

"Chase, you've got to hurry! There's no time!" Drake shouted.

"Working as fast as we can, Drake. Anything, Dunbar?"

Chase watched as the man punched in credentials for an officer whose name she didn't recognize, and then began his search for Craig Sloan. A moment later, an address appeared on screen.

"What the hell?"

"What?" Drake yelled through the phone. "What is it?"

"He... he lives in a halfway house in Jersey," Chase replied quietly.

"*Jersey?* You sure?"

"It says it right here — Craig Sloan, address in Jersey," Dunbar confirmed.

"No, that can't be right," Chase said, more to herself than to Drake or anyone else.

It didn't make sense. All of the murders had taken place in New York, and there was no way that he would risk taking both Suzan and Dr. Moorfield all the way to Jersey. Besides, if he grabbed Suzan this afternoon... did he take her to a safe place in Jersey first, then come back for Moorfield, only to go back again? Did he even have enough time to do all that?

Unless he's already killed Suzan...

Chase shook the thoughts from her head.

"Wait a second," she heard someone on the other end of the phone say. "Drake, quick, give me the phone... Chase? It's Beckett. There's no way this dude's in Jersey. He can't — wait a second!" Chase heard him snap his fingers, and when he spoke again, his voice was tight, excited. "Goddammit, it's the ashes! He's at the house that he burned down — tell me the address for that house!"

Chase tapped Dunbar on the shoulder.

"Gimme the address of the house Craig burned down."

Dunbar's fingers flew across the keys.

"It's in Lenox Hill."

"Lenox Hill? Did Dunbar say Lenox Hill?" Beckett cried.

"Lenox Hill," Chase confirmed.

"Then that's where he'll be."

Chase heard an engine rev in the background.

"I'm coming to meet you!" she shouted as she reached for her coat. "Be careful, for Christ's sake!"

But the line was already dead.

Chapter 64

DRAKE HAMMERED HIS CROWN Vic into drive and the car shot forward, clipping a chrome waste bin outside Ken Smith's condo complex.

"It's on East 70th," Beckett informed him out of the corner of his mouth. "You know where that is?"

Drake nodded enthusiastically.

"It's not far."

He yanked the wheel to the right and peeled out of the parking lot.

They had been driving for less than fifteen minutes before they saw the color of the sky change, transitioning from a deep navy to a caustic yellow.

We're too late, Drake thought. *I'm too late.*

"Fuck!"

He pushed the gas pedal all the way to the floor, swerving to avoid slower moving cars that became a blur, their blaring horns melting into a drone.

Drake pulled onto East 70th Street a few minutes later, the throaty growl of the Crown Vic now punctuated with a metallic sound, a tangible protest to having been pushed so hard.

But Drake barely heard any of this; the blood roared in his ears like an oceanic high tide.

Dr. Moorfield's house suddenly loomed into view and a moan escaped his lips.

"Jesus Christ," Beckett muttered from the passenger seat.

The entire second floor was ablaze, a kaleidoscope of intense yellow, orange, and red hues. The heat from the fire was so powerful that even from thirty feet away, the interior of the car suddenly felt like a sauna.

Ignoring the heat, Drake pulled into the driveway and leaped from the vehicle. Vaguely aware that Beckett was struggling to keep up, he sprinted down the side of the house, his aim set for the shadowy figure that he had seen climbing out of a window.

Heart thudding in his chest, Drake turned the corner just as he reached top speed.

The man wearing black never saw him coming.

Drake drove his shoulder into the unsuspecting man's spine, sending them both sprawling to the ground. Drake, breathing heavily, flipped the man over while raising a fist above his head.

"Where is she?" he bellowed.

The man looked up at him with wide eyes and horror washed over Drake. He recognized this man, their killer: it was the same man who had helped him up when he had fallen outside Barney's.

What had he said?

You should be careful out here, especially if you've been drinking... not everyone is as nice as I am.

The felled man took advantage of Drake's momentary confusion and shot a knee upward, into his groin.

Drake grunted as searing pain shot up from the point of impact, and his body protectively curled into a modified fetal position. Through flashes of red and white, Drake saw the man struggling to scramble to his feet. With a guttural roar, he fought the pain in his crotch and at the last moment managed to unfurl himself.

Drake's hand shot out and latched onto the man's ankle. Mustering all of his remaining strength, he pulled—pulled *hard*—and the man crashed back down. His hands went out to break his fall, but he was too slow and his chin bounced off the flagstones with a tremendous *smack*.

Drake crawled on top of him, grabbing a handful of his brown hair.

"Where is she?" he yelled again, feeling the heat from the burning house to his right beginning to scald his flesh.

There was no answer; the man had been knocked out cold.

Drake jumped to his feet and spun around, surprised to see Beckett standing behind him, a shocked expression on his face.

"Grab him! Throw him in the trunk!" Drake yelled.

Beckett, frozen in fear, just stood there.

"Do it!"

The second shout spurred Beckett to action and he strode forward, grabbing ahold of Craig Sloan's ankles.

"Where are you going?"

Drake turned to the burning house.

"Inside! I'm going inside! She could still be alive in there! Suzan could still be alive!"

Without waiting for a response, Drake shielded his face from the blaze, and then pulled himself through the opening in the plywood that moments before the killer had crawled out of.

Chapter 65

BECKETT WATCHED HIS FRIEND disappear into the flames. He wanted to stop him, to tell him that they were too late, that Suzan was gone, but he knew better than to waste his breath.

Drake was going to find Suzan Cuthbert, or he would die trying.

And it was all his fault. None of this would have happened if he hadn't asked Suzan to be his TA, to help him look into the strange coincidences between recent suicides and the forensic pathology final exam.

Tears streamed down his face, and Beckett ground his teeth. With a grunt, he dragged Craig's limp body down the side of the house. The man was thin, but Beckett wasn't used to this sort of physical exertion and within seconds, sweat mixed with the tears on his face.

Everything that had happened was so surreal, so completely outside his reality.

Puzzles... he liked puzzles, and most of the people he came across in his line of work were already dead. Heading to Montreal to inquire about a murder was one thing, but this... this was too much.

Beckett eventually dragged Craig's limp body to the front of the house. When he got to the Crown Vic, he reached inside and popped the trunk. Then he oriented Craig's body close to the opening. With a deep breath, he leaned down and scooped up his body. He teetered and for a brief moment, he feared that he was going to topple. Grinding his teeth and driving his feet into the asphalt, he managed to right himself, and with a final thrust, he managed to drop the man's body into the trunk.

Craig's body landed with a dull thud, and his eyes rolled back in his head. Beckett's eyes locked on the man's face, and it was suddenly the only thing that he could see.

The fire in front of him was gone, and he was deaf to the sirens that had started to fill the night air.

There was only him and their killer.

"Wake up!" he screamed. "Wake up! Wake up! *Wake up!*"

He wanted—no, wanted wasn't a strong enough word for what he felt. Beckett *needed* the man to atone for what he had done, for the lives he had destroyed, including his own.

"Wake up!" he shrieked.

Beckett was nearing hysteria now, and he might have lost it completely if it weren't for the sound of splitting wood from inside the house.

His eyes flicked up in time to see part of the roof collapse inward with an incredible shower of sparks.

Beckett slammed the trunk closed, avoiding looking at Craig again for fear of what might happen, and then pulled out his cell phone.

"Chase!" he yelled. "We need an ambulance and the fire department to Dr. Moorfield's house in Lenox Hill *now!*"

Chapter 66

DRAKE FOUND DR. TRACEY Moorfield on the stairs. The woman's gray hair had been burnt away, and her face was white with blisters. Her clothes were still smoldering, and in spots where it had burnt away completely, Drake saw blackened patches of flesh beneath.

"Where is she? Where's Suzan?" he shouted, trying to make himself heard over the roar of the fire.

The woman, who was crawling down the stairs, croaked but seemed to have lost the ability to form words.

Drake turned his attention to the upper level. It was clear by the intensity of the heat bearing down on him that this was where the fire had started.

And also the most likely place to find Suzan.

"Suzan!" he yelled. "Suzan, where are you!"

The woman on the stairs croaked again, but this time Drake thought he heard a single word on her charred tongue.

"Upstairs."

Drake leaped over Dr. Moorfield and took the stairs two at a time. With every step, the intensity of the heat increased, and he pulled the collar of his shirt up to his eyes to try and keep his flesh from burning, which also helped filter the acrid smoke that filled the air. And yet despite this measure, he could feel his mind start to swim, the lack of oxygen making him dizzy.

On the landing, he instinctively turned to his left. It was so hot now that Drake could no longer run forward; in fact, he couldn't even walk straight anymore. He was forced to turn sideways and lead with an outstretched hand, shuffling toward where he thought—where he hoped—Suzan might be.

"Suzan!" he yelled again, but this time the word was completely swallowed by the fire.

His eyes were watering, and he could feel the skin on his lead hand and forehead start to blister.

And yet his forward progress never stopped.

Drake found Suzan huddled in a ball toward the back of the house, in what he assumed had once been a bedroom.

"No!" he screamed. Upon seeing her body, all self-defense mechanisms went out the window. Drake sprinted toward Suzan, barely avoiding the melted mess of a jerry can, and then bent down and scooped her up. The smoke was so thick toward the back of the house, that he couldn't tell if she was injured, couldn't even tell if she was breathing.

It didn't matter.

Drake hoisted her thin body to his chest and then hurried back the way he had come.

Dr. Moorfield had since made it to the bottom of the stairs, but that was as far as she had gotten. She had collapsed in a motionless heap, blisters on her bare back hissing and popping like a demented organic orchestra.

Drake stepped over the corpse, and then his mind swirled and he almost went down. Gritting his teeth, he somehow managed to continue forward.

The cool night air was like ice water against his singed skin. The difference in temperature was so great that his body immediately seized and he fell to his knees.

Please don't die on me, Suzan. Please don't die on me. Please... Please... Please...

The last thing Drake heard before darkness overcame him was the sound of gunshots filling the night air.

Chapter 67

BECKETT INTENDED TO FOLLOW Drake into the house, but had only made it halfway—his progress had been slowed by several more collapsing sections of roof—when he heard the first gunshot.

He instinctively crouched, covering his head, turning toward the sound as he did.

More gunshots erupted, and Beckett saw about half a dozen bullet holes blossom on the trunk of Drake's Crown Vic.

He should have run. Every fiber of his being was telling him to turn and run, seek shelter from Craig Sloan and the fire by cowering a safe distance across the street.

But he didn't; something forced him to hold his ground. It might have been guilt, it might have been a bastardized form of bravery, or it might have been something else entirely.

Beckett didn't know.

But whatever it was, it drove him toward the car instead of away from it. Even when another shot rang out, this one shattering the lock on the hood, and a gloved hand tentatively gripped it from the inside, Beckett continued forward.

His foot collided with something, and he glanced down.

A baseball-sized stone wobbled across the driveway. Without thinking, Beckett bent to pick it up, then continued toward the car.

When he looked up, Craig Sloan had managed to swing a leg out of the hood. He was looking in the other direction and judging by the way his body swayed, it was clear that he was still feeling the effects of his chin cracking off the flagstones.

He clutched a pistol in his right hand, the black barrel nearly completely lost in the background of his black outfit.

Craig had only just managed to lift his body out of the trunk when Beckett came upon him.

"You killed her!" Beckett hissed.

Craig Sloan turned, a look of confusion on his face. Blood flowed from a thick gash on his chin, and when his lips parted in surprise at the sight of Beckett raising the stone, he revealed only shattered remnants of his top and bottom teeth.

Craig tried to bring the gun up, but Beckett's arm flew forward with remarkable speed.

There was a sickening, wet smack as the rock struck Craig Sloan in the temple. The man's eyes rolled back, and he staggered.

"You killed her," Beckett repeated, this time his voice barely a whisper.

He swung the rock again, and this time Craig dropped the gun.

"You killed her."

His hand shot forward a third time, sending a now unconscious Craig sprawling.

The rock came back soaked with blood, but this didn't stop him.

Nothing could stop Beckett now.

Chapter 68

DETECTIVE CHASE ADAMS WASN'T the first person on the scene, but when she arrived the entire street was gripped by pandemonium.

There were three fire trucks trying to put out the inferno, one of which had collided with an ambulance, causing the siren, which was still blaring, to fill the night sky with a high-pitched whine.

Chase leaped from her car and weaved her way through the four or five police cruisers already on scene.

A uniformed officer moved to stop her, but he must have realized who she was as he stepped out of her way before she shoved by him.

"Drake!" she hollered. "Drake!"

Her eyes skipped along all of the figures by the side of the road, trying to find an outline that matched Drake's.

A hand suddenly came down on her shoulder, and she whipped around, subconsciously balling her own hands into fists.

Detective Yasiv's young face stared back at her.

"He's fine," Yasiv said. "And Suzan's fine, too. She has some burns, pretty bad in some places, and she'll have to be on oxygen for a while, but she's going to pull through."

Chase felt her entire body start to tremble.

"Wh—wh—what? Are you sure?"

Yasiv nodded.

"They're going to be fine, Chase. Drake got here just in time."

Chase felt her eyes begin to water and knew that she was within seconds of her emotions overwhelming her. She pulled away from Detective Yasiv and started to backpedal.

"Chase? You okay?" he asked, the relief on his face morphing into concern.

Chase shook her head, and then turned and started to run—to run away from Detective Yasiv, Drake, Suzan, to run from everything.

Through tear-streaked vision, she sprinted toward a quiet alley between two abandoned houses far enough away to offer some relief from the heat of the fire, but still close enough to hear the damn wounded ambulance siren.

With one furtive glance over her shoulder to make sure she was alone, Chase melted. She collapsed to her knees and buried her hands in her face. The sobs came fast and furious.

They're alive! Somehow... they're alive!

They weren't tears of joy, not quite, but they weren't a result of sorrow or anguish, either.

They were from being overwhelmed, from being so close to losing *everything*.

A scraping sound caused her to pull her face from her hands.

"Who's there?" she hissed.

There was a flicker of movement in the shadows and Chase instinctively reached behind her and withdrew her gun.

Holding the pistol out in front of her, she rose to her feet and repeated the query.

"Who's there? Who the *fuck* is there?"

A man stepped from the shadows, and Chase's breath caught in her throat. She immediately lowered her gun.

"Beckett?" She squinted hard in the moonlight. It was indeed Beckett, but his face looked older somehow. Her eyes fell on his arms next, which were held out to his sides, and she immediately rushed toward him. "What the hell happened?"

Her first thought was that Beckett's sleeves had caught fire and that he had found water in this alley to soak them in, to extinguish the flames. But as she neared, she realized that it wasn't water that had darkened his jacket.

It was blood, and it coated him nearly to the elbows.

"He—he tried to get away," Beckett said in a faraway voice.

A large stone fell from his hand and clattered to the ground.

"What? Who?" Chase gasped.

Beckett swooned, and she grabbed him just before he went down.

"Who, Beckett? Who tried to get away?"

But then she saw *'who'*. Lying on the ground just ten paces behind Beckett was the body of a man dressed in black. Only it wasn't a complete silhouette. From the neck up, everything went flat, degenerating into a glistening pool of blood that painted the gravel walk.

"He had a gun and—"

Chase pulled away from Beckett. Then she reached up and grabbed the man's face with both hands. Initially, his eyes didn't focus, and she dug her nails into his skin until his gaze fixed on hers.

"Listen to me, Beckett. Did he have a gun?"

Beckett nodded, and Chase kept her grip firm.

"Where is it?"

"I—I don't know, it was in the trunk, and then..." he shrugged. "I don't know what happened to it."

Chase frowned and she squeezed his cheeks even harder.

"Think, Beckett. *Think!*"

Beckett's eyelids fluttered, and this time Chase slapped him across the face.

"Think!"

Lucidity returned to Beckett's eyes.

"He dropped it," he said at last. "He dropped it by the car."

Chase ground her teeth.

"Alright, listen to me, Beckett. Here's what we're going to do…"

Chapter 69

CHASE STOOD OVER THE hospital bed, peering down at Drake as he slept. His head was covered in bandages, and he had gauze pads glued to both of his cheeks.

All in all, though, he didn't look that bad. In fact, she had seen him look worse. According to the medic who had treated him at the scene, and the doctor Chase had spoken to just moments ago, all of his wounds were superficial. He'd have some sore hands due to the burns, and his face was going to get redder before it returned to its normal color, but nothing was permanent.

All Drake needed was rest and oxygen, and he would be back on his feet in no time.

"Is she... is she alive?"

Drake's words, muffled by the oxygen mask that covered his nose and mouth, startled her. He pulled the mask off, wincing at the pain in his hands.

"Is she alive?" He asked again.

Chase looked down at him, tears starting to form in her eyes.

"Suzan's going to be fine, Drake. You got to her just in time."

Drake's face seemed to collapse in on itself and he started to weep.

"Dr. Moorfield didn't cut her throat," Chase continued. "She cut her here, on the scalp," she ran a finger behind her ear and then moved downward. "Lots of blood, but no real damage."

Chase debated telling her ex-partner what had happened to Beckett, but decided against it. A man in his position could only handle so much at one time.

Drake wiped the tears from his face with his bandaged hands and then started to sit up.

"Woah, woah! You can't get up, Drake."

"I need to see her," he said gruffly.

Chase shook her head.

"You can't. She's in a protected oxygen room to help clear her lungs and deal with her burns. But she's going to be fine."

Drake swung his legs over the side of the bed and then paused.

"What about Dr. Moorfield?"

Chase's heart sunk as she remembered the scene outside the burning house, the paramedics working hard on Tracey Moorfield's blackened body.

She shook her head.

"Dr. Moorfield didn't make it. She died from asphyxiation."

Drake frowned.

"And Craig Sloan? Is he in custody."

Chase's frown deepened. Drake was too smart, too intuitive, to be left in the dark about anything, it seemed. And yet she felt a nagging urge to spare the man the details of the scene she had witnessed between the two abandoned houses.

He—he tried to get away... he had a gun.

"He isn't in custody, is he?"

Chase shook her head.

"No. He's not."

Drake suddenly became agitated and he rocketed to his feet. The tubing extending from the IV embedded in the back of his right hand snagged, and he wobbled. She went to him, but he shrugged her off and yanked the line from his hand.

"Drake, Craig's dead. There was an... altercation and he was killed."

Drake got a far-off look in his eyes.

"I heard the shots," he said quietly, followed by a subtle nod. "And Beckett? Is Beckett okay?"

"He's fine. Shaken up, for sure, but he'll pull through. You'd know better than I, but Beckett doesn't strike me as the type of man to be kept down for long."

Drake seemed to relax, and he took a deep breath. This reprieve only lasted a few seconds, however. His eyes darted around the room.

"My clothes? Where are my clothes?"

"I really think you should lie back down, Drake. You've been through hell."

He shook his head.

"You don't know the half of it. But there is still something I have to do. Do you know where my clothes are?"

"They were burnt; they've been tossed."

Drake swore under his breath, his eyes turning to the oversized scrubs that the nurse had helped him into after he had been admitted.

"But I brought you something clean to wear," Chase admitted with a sigh, knowing that she wasn't going to be able to convince him to stay put. She reached into the large bag on the chair behind her and handed it to Drake.

He looked inside and then smiled at her.

"Ol' trusty, huh?"

She shrugged.

"I figured you'd want to be comfortable."

Drake pulled out a white shirt, followed by a pair of pants. Last to come out of the bag was his worn sport coat.

"You sure I can't convince you to stay and rest?" Chase said as a last-ditch effort.

Drake looked at her then, an incredible sadness in his eyes. It was only then that she realized just how damaged he was, how deeply Clay's death had affected him.

Tears began to form in her eyes again.

Even though Drake was the one who had saved Suzan, and without him, she would have almost certainly become the suicide killer's seventh victim, a part of Chase regretted showing up at Triple D that day.

Drake, misinterpreting her expression, suddenly embraced her. Chase's eyes went wide with surprise, and she hesitated before hugging him back.

"Thank you," he whispered softly in her ear.

And then, without another word, Drake was gone, leaving Chase alone in the hospital room with only her thoughts.

Chapter 70

Beckett awoke with a start.

He blinked hard, trying to clear his vision, while at the same time trying to figure out where the hell he was.

He remembered the sound of gunshots, the crackle of a fire. *Was it fireworks? Was I at some sort of festival?*

But then an image of a trunk peppered with bullet holes, of a man's leg sticking out of it, came to him, and with that everything else flooded back.

Beckett sat bolt upright and looked around, tightness gripping his narrow chest. He was in a room of sorts, a small, square room with beige walls that reminded him of a hospital room. There was a cream-colored sheet pulled up to his chin, and he flipped it off. He moved to rise when the sound of metal on metal drew his attention to his wrist.

He was handcuffed to the metal gurney.

"Stay calm, Beckett," a voice said softly from his right.

Beckett's eyes flicked in that direction, and he squinted hard.

"Screech? That you? What am I doing here? Am I under arrest?"

Screech stepped forward.

"Quiet, we have to be quick," the man said, holding a piece of paper out to him. Beckett took it with his free hand.

"Have to be quick? Why? What's going on?"

Screech's frown deepened.

"Just read the damn thing and memorize it. Chase says all you have to do is recite it to them when they come to interview you."

Them?

His mind was suddenly flooded with flashes of images, like a poorly edited film. A stone being pulled back, then driving forward before being retracted again. With each successive blow, it came back redder and wetter.

Beckett shook his head and scanned the short paragraph on the page he held in a trembling hand. When he was done, he handed it back to Screech.

"That's it?"

Screech nodded.

"That's it. Did you memorize it?"

Beckett said that he had.

"Good," Screech replied, shoving the paper into his jean pocket. Then he waved a hand dramatically in front of his face. "Alright, I'm going to David Blaine on your ass now—I was never here. *Poof!*"

Then Screech turned to leave, but at the last moment, he lowered a hand on Beckett's shoulder.

"I'd have done the same thing, Beckett. Just stick to the script and we'll be having a drink together soon, okay?"

The man offered a weak smile, and Beckett did his best to return it.

With that, Screech made his way to the door. He knocked once, and Officer Dunbar's face suddenly appeared in the rectangular window. A second later, the door opened and Screech vanished.

Chapter 71

THE AIR WAS CHILLY, and Drake got the impression that it wouldn't be long before the first snowfall descended on New York like a frigid plague.

He sat in his Crown Vic, the windows open, enjoying the cool air on his burned skin. His eyes trained on the apartment building, he waited.

After about an hour, the door opened and Steff Morgan stepped out. She had a backpack slung over one shoulder and she walked briskly, with purpose. Pulling her coat up to her ears, she looked both ways before hurrying down the sidewalk.

Only when she was out of sight did Drake get out of his car. Like Steff, his stride was determined, but unlike her, he headed toward the apartment and not away from it.

After briefly glancing around to make sure that the street was quiet, he raised his gauzed hand to knock on the door. At the last second, he decided against it and instead kicked it with his boot.

He heard stirring from inside the building, but when the footsteps didn't sound as if they were any nearer to the door, he kicked again.

And again.

"I'm coming. Hold your horses," a muffled male voice replied.

Drake stopped kicking and waited. He heard the deadbolt turn and then locked his eyes on the door handle. When it started to turn, he shoved the door open.

The man standing behind the door cried out and stumbled backward. Drake was on him before he managed to raise his hands defensively.

He grabbed the man by the throat and threw him up against the wall. As he tightened his grip, he felt blisters pop beneath the bandages, but paid this no heed.

"If you hit her again, I will kill you," he said simply.

Jake was making a strange hissing sound with his mouth, and spit speckled Drake's face.

He relaxed his grip and when Jake fell away from the wall, his mouth opened in an attempt to speak.

Drake threw Jake against the wall again, the back of his head smacking against the drywall hard enough to leave a dent.

"If you hit her again, I'll kill you," he repeated.

This time, Jake didn't say anything.

Drake let go of the man's throat and he collapsed to the ground, wheezing. Then he left the apartment and didn't look back.

***

"Jesus Christ, Drake—what the hell happened to you?" Mickey asked from behind the bar.

Drake didn't answer as he made his way toward the man. He gestured with a bandaged hand and the bartender quickly poured him a glass of whiskey.

"It's been a long day, Mickey. A long, *long* day."

Mickey didn't bother trying to hide his discomfort at Drake's appearance.

"No kidding. It looks like you fought a fireplace and lost—*badly*."

Drake sipped his drink.

"Something like that."

"Well, shit, the drink's on the house."

Drake took another gulp of the golden liquid, wincing at how the alcohol stung his raw throat.

"Thanks," he grumbled.

After drinking in silence for several minutes, Drake realized that he was unable to let his mind roam free, to block out the events of the past week.

For once, even the alcohol didn't seem to be helping.

There was, however, something that he thought might be able to take his mind off things, if only for a short while.

"Hey, Mickey?"

The bartender turned to face him.

"What's up? Need a refill?"

Drake looked down at his glass.

"Yes, but I need something else, too. Have you heard from Alyssa, lately?"

Mickey smirked.

"Naw, she rarely comes in here. Not her usual clientele, if you know what I mean."

Drake frowned.

"Clientele?"

"Yeah, she usually works the more upscale joints in Manhattan. In fact, I haven't seen her since the night she left with you."

Drake couldn't believe his ears.

"Wh—what? What do you mean clientele?"

The smile fell off Mickey's face and he left the customers at the end of the bar and came over to him.

Leaning in close, he said, "You know, rich kids."

"No, I don't know. What the hell are you talking about?"

Mickey stared him directly in the face for several seconds before speaking.

"Shit, I'm sorry, Drake. I thought you knew. Alyssa's a call girl."

Drake felt his body deflate.

A call girl? I slept with a prostitute?

Drake looked down and sighed.

"It's alright," he said as he finished his whiskey.

It made sense, what with her coming home with him and staying the night, then sneaking out before he was awake, not bothering to leave her number.

He had had his suspicions, of course. But if Alyssa was a call girl, why hadn't she asked for any payment?

But Drake realized that he knew the answer to that as well.

Alyssa hadn't asked for money because she had already been paid. And there was only one person he knew who would throw that kind of money around to get what he wanted.

And in this case, what *he* wanted was Drake.

"Sorry, Drake," Mickey said again, before sliding down the bar to deal with a couple who had just taken a seat at the neon bar.

Drake pulled out his cell phone and intended to click on his contacts, but the booze and exhaustion took its toll and he missed his mark.

Instead, he clicked on the app that looked like a video camera.

"Fuck," he said, meaning to back out to the home screen. But when the video loaded, he saw something that caught his eye.

It was the familiar view of Mrs. Armatridge's house divided into four quadrants.

In the upper right-hand corner was the Armatridge's bed, the covers were pulled up high. Only it wasn't freshly made.

There was movement from beneath the sheets. A *lot* of movement.

A tanned arm slipped out of the sheets and then proceeded to pull them up higher.

"What the hell?" he whispered.

A flurry of activity drew his attention to the lower left-hand corner: the kitchen. Mrs. Armatridge was at the knife block again, and as he watched, she pulled a large blade from the wood.

She looked at it for a second, nodded, then started toward the stairs.

"*What the hell?*" he repeated, more loudly this time.

When Mrs. Armatridge made it to the stairs, Drake realized what was happening, what the woman was intending to do.

"*What the hell!*"

He flicked to the home screen, then went scrolled to his contacts. Only instead of calling Ken Smith as he had first intended, he dialed Screech instead.

"Screech! You need to—"

"Drake, that you? Are you okay? I meant to—"

"Screech, just listen. You need to head to Mrs. Armatridge's place right now!"

"What? What the hell are you talking—"

"Just shut the fuck up for once, and just go, Screech! Get off your ass and *go!*"

Drake hung up the phone, still in shock at what he had seen.

For some reason, his mind turned to what Mrs. Armatridge had said the first time they had met, which had oddly mimicked what Dr. Mark Kruk had said long ago.

People see what they want to see. They don't really see what's there. An imago.

Epilogue

"IN HERE," CHASE SAID to the two men in the freshly pressed suits. The men didn't bother knocking on the office door. They simply turned the knob and entered.

Chase smiled.

"Hey! What do you think you're doing?" Rhodes shouted, jumping to his feet.

Chase stepped into the office behind the two men.

"Check his desk; the photographs are in the top drawer."

The taller of the two men nodded at her and then walked around to Rhodes's side of the desk.

"What the fuck do you think you're doing?" Rhodes repeated, his face turning a deep shade of crimson.

"Officers Lincoln and Herd, Internal Affairs," the shorter man said, his face stern.

Rhodes blinked once, his Adam's apple bobbed, and he started toward the door.

The man who had executed the perfunctory introduction pointed a short finger at Rhodes's chest.

"Stay where you are, Sergeant Rhodes."

Rhodes looked like he was going to explode. He stared daggers at Chase.

"Did you bring these guys in? You brought *IA* in?" he demanded, his voice nearing a hysterical pitch.

Chase shrugged and said nothing.

Officer Lincoln pulled a manila folder from the top drawer of his desk and placed it on top. He opened it, and then held up the first photograph for Chase to see.

"This it?"

She nodded.

"Yeah, that's it."

Lincoln tucked the folder into his briefcase.

"What's the meaning of this?"

"Oh, I think you know, Rhodes. I brought this to your attention twice and you ignored it. Now we have a prestigious professor burned alive, and the daughter of a murdered policeman in the hospital. So maybe, just maybe, you should have listened to me," Chase said, not bothering to hide the smugness that crept into her voice.

"What? *What?* Who?"

"Dr. Moorfield had some important friends, Rhodes. And when they heard what happened to her, they were curious as to why nothing was being done about the serial killer that took her life."

Rhodes gawked.

"Serial killer?"

Chase was done with this conversation. She turned to Lincoln.

"That should be enough."

The man nodded.

"Sergeant Rhodes, you are officially suspended pending an investigation into your lack of action in this case."

Now Rhodes really looked like he was about to erupt. But his eyes glanced nervously at Lincoln and then Herd, and in the end, he decided better than shouting.

Instead, he bowed his head, and slowly, methodically, walked by Chase and left the office without another word.

"Hey Rhodes," Chase hollered after him. "You said you wouldn't be Sergeant for long, but I bet this wasn't what you had in mind, was it?"

END

Author's note

I've spent the past 13 years studying pathology, and yet I'm not afraid to admit that there is still so much I don't know. Which is why I couldn't write this book without help. So what did I do? Well, I did what any sane, rational person would: I sent an innocuous email to an old pathologist colleague of mine. It went a little like this: 'Hi Sara, hope you and yours are doing well. Just wondering, if I wanted to kill someone and make it look like a suicide or accident, how might I go about it?'

Thank you, Sara, for not immediately calling the police. And thank you for all of your help with Cause of Death. I couldn't have finished it without you.

Also, for the record, you apparently can't electrocute someone with a car battery. The method I described in the book, however, is highly plausible. But, truth be told, I haven't tested it and don't intend to anytime soon. I know, I know, the movies lied to us. You also can't ignite gasoline with a cigarette. Another lie.

Bastards.

When I started the Detective Damien Drake Series, I wanted to write something raw, real, and full of characters with complicated problems. With Butterfly Kisses, I knew Beckett was going to be a recurring character, but given the subject matter of Cause of Death, it only made sense that his involvement would increase. But even I had no idea that he was going to go off the rails the way he did at the end of the book. I won't lie; Beckett intrigues me greatly. I'm always looking for characters working in professions who don't really fit the stereotype, the mold. Kinda like me. Thirteen years becoming a doctor and studying pathology, and now I write novels. *Whodathunk* it.

Thanks for coming along on this journey with me. I'm happy to say that it's only just begun. Plenty of books on the horizon, more murders to solve. *Always* more murders.

You keep reading, and I'll keep on writing.

Best,
Patrick
Montreal, 2017